Logan and Dora threw their car doors open and ran for the wreck...

Tires screeched as drivers came to abrupt stops on the street behind them, and screams filled the air.

The front of the suspect's car had folded like an accordion.

Dora reached through the driver's side window and pressed two fingers against the side of the driver's neck. There was a pulse, a faint one, but it was there.

"He's alive." Dora pulled her hand back. "Call for an ambulance."

Her legs gave out, and she went down onto her knee. It was then that she realized that she was bleeding, as well.

"Dora!" Logan was beside her in an instant.

She pressed a hand to her side and pulled it back bloody. A wave of dizziness hit her.

KILLER ON THE POTOMAC

K.D. RICHARDS

Harlequin
INTRIGUE

If you purchased this book without a cover you should be aware that this book is stolen property. It was reported as "unsold and destroyed" to the publisher, and neither the author nor the publisher has received any payment for this "stripped book."

Harlequin® INTRIGUE™

ISBN-13: 978-1-335-69022-7

Killer on the Potomac

Copyright © 2025 by Kia Dennis

All rights reserved. No part of this book may be used or reproduced in any manner whatsoever without written permission.

Without limiting the author's and publisher's exclusive rights, any unauthorized use of this publication to train generative artificial intelligence (AI) technologies is expressly prohibited.

This is a work of fiction. Names, characters, places and incidents are either the product of the author's imagination or are used fictitiously. Any resemblance to actual persons, living or dead, businesses, companies, events or locales is entirely coincidental.

For questions and comments about the quality of this book, please contact us at CustomerService@Harlequin.com.

TM and ® are trademarks of Harlequin Enterprises ULC.

Harlequin Enterprises ULC
22 Adelaide St. West, 41st Floor
Toronto, Ontario M5H 4E3, Canada
www.Harlequin.com

Printed in Lithuania

Recycling programs for this product may not exist in your area.

MIX
Paper | Supporting responsible forestry
FSC® C021394

K.D. Richards is a native of the Washington, DC, area, who now lives outside Toronto with her husband and two sons. You can find her at kdrichardsbooks.com.

Books by K.D. Richards

Harlequin Intrigue

Guardians of Justice

Killer on the Potomac

West Investigations

Pursuit of the Truth
Missing at Christmas
Christmas Data Breach
Shielding Her Son
Dark Water Disappearance
Catching the Carling Lake Killer
Under the Cover of Darkness
A Stalker's Prey
Silenced Witness
Lakeside Secrets
Under Lock and Key
The Perfect Murder

Visit the Author Profile page at Harlequin.com.

CAST OF CHARACTERS

Detective Dora Madison—Heroine and DC police detective.

Agent Logan Elkins—FBI profiler and Dora's ex-boyfriend.

Detective Wendell Keene—Dora's partner.

Randi Singer—Witness to the most recent murder.

Lieutenant Tracy Crenshaw—Dora's supervisor.

Chapter One

It was nearly five in the morning. He'd gotten a much later start than he'd planned, but the moon hid behind clouds still shrouding the city park in near darkness as he pulled into the empty lot and cut his engine. He'd done his homework and knew that the two cameras hanging high above on either end of the lot had long ceased to work. He'd broken the bulb in the lone streetlight two nights earlier and was relieved to see the city had yet to switch it for a new one.

"Everything's coming up roses," he sang softly.

He continued humming the tune as he got out of the car, opened the trunk, and lifted the body out of it. He cradled it close as he made his way along the path. Fallen leaves swirled in a breeze. He'd scouted the location extensively and knew exactly where he was headed. He passed the playground and the basketball courts and stepped onto the soft grass in the open field, passing an empty picnic table. The night was unusually balmy, and they were due for rain, but the ground was hard and dry now. He'd chosen her final resting place well.

He wished this one had been the one. He'd been searching for so long and had finally thought he'd found her. His Sarah. But once again, he'd been wrong. He hadn't thought it would be so difficult.

When he arrived at his chosen spot, he lowered the body to the ground. He took his time positioning her, then snapped a photo with the phone that only he knew about. Even though she wasn't the one he was looking for, she was still so beautiful. It almost hurt to leave her. But he knew he couldn't stay. He needed to move quickly. The last thing he wanted was to be spotted by some vagrant or early-morning jogger running through the park. He had to be long gone, preferably back home and in his bed, when the body was found.

A sliver of moon broke through the cloud-covered sky, casting a glowing light on the body. He couldn't help himself; he knew he should leave. Instead, he crouched down, fluffing the hair he'd fanned out around her and running his fingers over her cheek and down the side of her neck one last time. "I'm sorry we couldn't be together forever. I will miss you."

He'd have to keep searching. The thought made him smile as he turned and walked back along the path to his car, humming his favorite song.

Chapter Two

A 6:00 a.m. summons to a crime scene gave new meaning to the saying "Mondays are murder," Detective Dora Madison thought as she drove to the small park nestled in the Adams Morgan neighborhood in Washington, DC. It was rare to get a call out to this area, much less one about a body found in the park. The city's homicide rate had been trending downward for several years, but in the last month she'd caught two homicides that had a grown a hole in the pit of her stomach. From the scant details that the dispatcher had given her about the crime scene, that hole was about to get deeper.

Half a dozen police cruisers blocked the park's entrance when she arrived. She paused in front of the baby-faced officer, flashed her badge, and made her way back along an asphalt walkway that passed by a playground, a softball field, and a basketball court to her crime scene. She slipped her hands into nitrile gloves as she made her way down the path. There was a buzz of activity—forensics techs and more uniformed officers—on the open lawn to her right, about fifty feet off the path. Yellow police tape wound around a tree, to a picnic table, around a stick that someone had seen fit to plunge into the ground and back to the tree, forming a misshapen triangle around the body lying on the dew-covered grass.

A red-faced man with dark, hair and a Mediterranean brown complexion strode toward her. He wore a tired black suit, off the rack, a white shirt, a striped blue-and-white tie, and well-worn loafers. His eyes were dark and grim, and his lips were pressed together into a harsh line. She recognized him as a detective out of the Third District, which usually caught all the cases originating in the Adams Morgan neighborhood, but for the life of her, she couldn't remember his name.

He reached for her and extended his hand. "Detective Madison? I'm Detective Wendell Keene." His glove-clad handshake was firm. Keene looked to be in his early thirties, with short brown hair cut in a fashion that told her he'd been in the military. He was only slightly taller than her five feet, ten inches, but he carried himself with a confidence that couldn't be taught.

"Nice to meet you, albeit under these less-than-ideal circumstances," Dora said. "What do we have?"

Keene turned on his heel, and together they walked toward the body, Keene reading from the small notebook in his hand. "Dispatch took a call at approximately five forty this morning. A jogger the park encountered a woman running from the direction of the body. She was visibly upset and said there was a body on the other side of the park. The jogger called 911, and officers were dispatched. They found a woman, late teens or early twenties, deceased." Keene looked up from his notes. "The officers immediately noted the flower in the victim's hair."

Dora let out a deep sigh. "Which is why I was called."

Keene nodded. "Yes. I got the call because that's standard operating procedure, but my lieutenant instructed me to bring you in immediately."

She was sure he had. The press was already grumbling about the rise in crime and the possibility of a serial killer stalking the streets of the nation's capital. It had been plain bad luck that she'd caught the first murder, a grocery store cashier with a flower in her hair. The second victim, a waitress, had been found three weeks later in the same neighborhood, although one of Dora's colleagues had been on duty when that call came in. Both victims were brunettes with slim, athletic builds and were in their early twenties. Once they had confirmed that the second victim had the same flower in her hair, their boss, Lieutenant Tracy Crenshaw, had made Dora the lead detective in both cases. Crenshaw was as close to a mentor as Dora had. The lieutenant had made it through the ranks at record speed, traversing all the diplomatic stuff as well as men who still had problems with women on the force, especially those reaching for rank. But Crenshaw had managed it all and was clearly still on her way up. She'd seen something in Dora and given her a shot, and more than anything Dora wanted to prove that the lieutenant's faith in her wasn't misplaced. Too often lately, she'd felt like she was failing.

And now they had a third victim. Official serial-killer territory. Although she doubted very much, she'd hear those two words cross Lieutenant Crenshaw's lips.

Solve this fast. I'm counting on you had been Lieutenant Crenshaw's exact words when she'd dropped the second case onto Dora's desk, but apparently Dora wasn't moving fast enough. Crenshaw had been on her for the last week, demanding daily, sometimes twice daily, updates on cases. It was becoming harder and harder to spin bupkis into something that sounded hopeful.

"Where are the jogger and the woman who found the body?"

"I had officers take them both to the Third District station. I can have them transported to you at the Sixth if you'd prefer to interview them there."

Dora shook her head. "No. I'll swing by the Third when we're finished here."

A forensic technician stepped aside as she and Keene approached the body. Dora examined the body with practiced eyes for several long moments. The young woman was on her back, her eyes vacantly gazing at the leafy tree branches above her. The woman's chocolate-brown hair fanned out around her head, and twigs and a leaf entwined in its strands, but the glossy sheen of her professional blowout was still ascertainable. Her face was made up—black mascara, gold sparkly eyeshadow, expertly applied and blended foundation, and the remains of what would have been a vibrant red lipstick clinging to her lips. The makeup seemed too heavy for a day at the office. It was more likely their victim had been out or was about to go out on a night out on the town. Her clothing confirmed that assessment. Black skintight leather pants with a sparkly gold top and strappy high-heeled sandals that looked more like torture devices than shoes.

"What happened to you?" Dora murmured, circling the body.

"Cause of death?"

"We don't know. There are no signs of trauma on the body."

Just as with the other victims. If this was the same killer, they'd find that this woman, like the others, had been drowned, most likely in a bathtub, while she'd been sedated. "Have you started a search of the park?"

"We have officers fanned out, searching the park and two blocks in each direction right now."

Dora stared off beyond the trees. This was a mixed residential and commercial area, with mostly apartments and condos. That meant many people were coming and going.

"Do we know when the body was placed here?" Because she was sure forensics would determine the victim had been placed just like the other two victims.

"Not yet."

She fought to hold back a frown. "Have we found any evidence at all?"

Keene's voice held more than a hint of irritation. "Still looking. There are multiple entrances to this park. No gates, although there are signs informing the public that the park is closed after dark."

Yeah, Dora was sure that did absolutely nothing to keep people out of the park at night.

"You came from the west entrance, so you know there's a parking lot there," Keene continued. "Whoever left her could have parked in the lot and carried her here."

"Possible." Dora frowned. "But he or she would have had to be strong."

"Or they could have used something to make the trip easier," Keene responded. "We've had a few dry days. The ground is hard. I've got uniforms looking for any sign of a vehicle or drag marks, but it might not be possible to discern any from the general wear and tear in the park."

That was always the trouble with a crime scene in a public place. So many people came through that it was nearly impossible to figure out what was evidence and what wasn't. Something their perpetrator obviously knew.

"Cameras?"

Keene shot her a forlorn look. "Two in the parking lot, but..."

She didn't need him to finish the sentence to know its ending. "They aren't working."

He shook his head. "Haven't been for more than a year."

It was long enough for anyone who lived in the area—heck, even many who didn't—to know.

"Let's assume our killer brought the victim in through the west entrance. It's the closest, and it makes the most sense based on what we know now. That means he or she could have been in and out of here in, what, ten minutes?"

Keene shrugged. "Maybe less. I think it's safe to say our guy scouts his dump sights and he—"

"Or she," Dora interjected.

"Or she, although female serials are less common," Keene added.

"I think both our commanding officers would have your head for uttering the *S*-word, but point taken."

"Our perp," Keene continued, opting for the safest description of their killer, "appears to be organized and has his or her crimes well thought out."

"I agree. And if their pattern holds, we'll find that our victim has been missing for three days." Dora stared at the body. The woman had been well groomed, her clothes were designer, her hair done in a salon or at least by someone who'd known what they were doing. Not the type of person who could typically go missing for three days without someone knowing. "Three days. We need to be looking at missing person's reports."

"Already got someone on it," Keene said.

"Make sure to expand the search into Northern Virginia and Maryland. We'll start with the DMV, but it's possible she came into the city from farther away." The

DMV, as it was affectionately called by those who lived in the area, was the region surrounded by Interstate 495 also known as the Beltway—although its borders were constantly shifting outward as the suburbs expanded and more and more people found it palatable to commute to the city from farther away.

"Got it," Keene answered.

She nodded toward the pathway that jutted from the one she'd used to trek from the parking lot to the crime scene where the apartment buildings stretched over the tops of the trees. "We need to canvass every unit in those apartment buildings."

Keene groaned.

Dora answered with a shrug. It would be a pain, but... "That's what uniforms are for. Someone might have seen something that puts us on our killer's tail. Or our killer could live in one of those buildings."

It wasn't out of the question. Most killers stayed close to home. It was one of the reasons some killers were so hard to catch. Their friends and neighbors just never thought of them as a killer.

Dora squatted next to the body. The woman's hands had been crossed one over the other and placed between her breasts. Her legs were similarly crossed at the ankle. Just like the first two victims. She touched the dead woman's forearm. It was stiff. "Rigor has set in. She's been dead for at least twenty-four hours."

"She hasn't been here for twenty-four hours. No way she wouldn't have been noticed."

"No." Dora got to her feet. "She hasn't been here that long. Hopefully, the canvass will give us a better idea about the much use this park gets." She made a mental note to question the jogger who'd called in the body too. How many people usually walked or jogged the path? Were there more in the mornings or the evenings? Was it a frequent lunchtime spot for workers in the area? "She was most likely placed here in the wee hours of this morning when the body would have still been flexible enough for her killer to pose like this. But that also leads me to believe our guy—"

"Or gal," Keene interjected with a mirthless smile.

"*Or gal* knows something about forensic science."

Their killer was smart. College educated, maybe. Or maybe he or she was just very skilled at killing. Just because they only had three bodies didn't mean their killer had only killed three people. She could be running even further behind than she'd realized.

Dora scanned the body as thoroughly as she could without touching it. No scratches on the skin were visible. The polish on her nails was chipped, but the nails themselves remained intact. There were no defensive wounds that Dora could see. If this woman had been drowned, she'd likely been sedated first, just like the other two victims.

"Have you had any luck running down the flower?" Keene asked.

"No." The single word came out as a growl, but Dora's frustration wasn't aimed at Keene as much as the situation. She'd never given much thought to flowers, but there were over four hundred thousand species of flowers and several dozen garden centers and nurseries in the DC metropolitan area. She'd keep pushing on the lead, but their perp could have gotten the flower from almost anywhere.

Keene cleared his throat. "I know it's your case, but if you wouldn't mind, I'd like to stay on."

She studied him for a moment before nodding. "I could

use all the help I can get. I think this one is going to take its toll before it's wrapped up."

"I've already put a call in to the medical examiner," he said. "He should be here soon to pick up the body. Would you mind if I observe the autopsy with you?"

Observing autopsies was one of her least favorite parts of the job, but they often revealed information and leads that were vital to catching a killer. "Sure. Why don't you stay on top of that and let me know when the medical examiner has it scheduled?"

Keene glanced down at the body once more. "What kind of sicko does something like this?"

Twelve years on the force and she didn't have an answer for him. "Let's check with the uniforms, see if they've turned up—"

As if he'd heard the words she'd been speaking, a baby-faced officer jogged around the bend in the pathway, a large plastic evidence bag in his hands. "Detectives!"

Dora approached the officer, with Keene at her side. His breastplate gave his last name as King. "Officer King, have you got something for us?"

Officer King held out the evidence bag. Inside, there was a small black purse encrusted with rhinestones. "Found this about a quarter mile away in some bushes. I got the techs to take photos before I bagged it."

"Good work, Officer," Keene said, taking the bag and carefully opening it.

Whether it was a natural male aversion to going through a woman's purse or because she was the lead detective, Keene passed the purse to Dora.

The usual necessities for a night out were inside: Lipstick. Cell phone. A hair tie. And a wallet. Dora snapped open the wallet and slid the driver's license out of the first slot.

Michelle Quitoni.

Dora passed the license to Keene, and the hole in her stomach opened into a chasm.

"Quitoni. Like that senator who has been all over the news lately?"

Dora slid the photograph that was in the slot behind the driver's license out. "Not *like* that senator. That senator's daughter." She held the photograph so that she and Keene could study it together. Senator Preston Quitoni and the woman lying in the field just feet from them smiled back at them.

Chapter Three

It was just after two in the afternoon when Special Agent Logan Elkins found himself pausing outside of the conference room at the Sixth District station where the chief of police, the deputy chief of police, the deputy mayor, and the lead detective on the case he'd just been assigned to waited for him. The main players were all different now. It had been over seven years since he'd left the Metropolitan Police Department, so that was to be expected. The MPD, as it was colloquially called, had a storied history. The department was more than a hundred and fifty years old, making it one of the oldest in the country. It was in a unique position, being a police department in a federal city, but it was still the primary policing authority in the area with law enforcement professionals who were second to none.

What he hadn't counted on was the bout of nerves he'd been fighting since pulling into the police parking lot. He couldn't remember the last time he'd been nervous walking into a meeting about a case, but it wasn't the case that had him on edge. It was seeing Detective Dora Madison again. The last time they'd spoken, over two years ago now, it had not gone well. He'd known his reassignment back to DC and her promotion to detective meant it was possible that their professional paths might cross at some point. Washington, DC, might have been the nation's capital, but it had a lot in common with small towns. But he and Dora were both professionals with a common goal: getting a killer off the streets.

He straightened his back, squared his shoulders, and reached for the conference room door. All the heads in the room turned toward him as he strode through the door. Despite his little pep talk in the hall, he scanned the faces for Dora and let out a sigh that was part relief and part disappointment when he realized she wasn't among the people in the room.

The chief stood up from his position at the head of the long, rectangular table that dominated the space and came forward. Chief of Police Stefon Bayne was a short African American man with a stocky build and, if rumors were true, a Napoleon complex. He wore his dress blues along with a scowl. "Special Agent Elkins," he said crisply, thrusting out his hand. "Thank you for coming."

"Of course. I'm happy to do whatever I can." The chief's hand was sweaty enough that Logan had to fight the urge to wipe his hand on his pant leg when the man let go.

"I understand you used to be part of the Metropolitan Police Department."

"It's been a few years, but I started my career here before moving on to the FBI."

"Well, we're happy to have you back helping on this case," Bayne answered, sounding anything but happy to have his help.

Murder, including serial murders, fell under the purview of the local police. The Federal Bureau of Investigation provided help, usually profiling and forensic work and occasionally manpower, when requested by the locals.

But Chief Bayne hadn't requested the FBI's help. Senator Quitoni had insisted the FBI be brought in to assist. That made the situation awkward, to say the least. But it wasn't the first time Logan had been tasked to work with hostile locals, and it wouldn't be the last time. He'd use this meeting to work out the power dynamics among the group—who he could sway to his side, who he could trust, and who he couldn't.

He cataloged the names and titles of each of the people in the room as they introduced themselves. The deputy chief of police, Tina Linuesa, and two of her aides. The deputy mayor, Carl Simone, with one aide. An attorney from the US Attorney's Office for the District of Columbia. A police press officer. The mayor's press officer. There were too many politicians and administrators and not enough of the people who were going to be doing the real work of finding a killer.

He was just about to ask if the detectives assigned to the case were going to be joining them when the conference room door opened.

"Ah, perfect timing, Lieutenant Crenshaw," Chief Bayne said with a disapproving frown. "We were just about to get started, Detectives."

"Sorry we're late. Got stuck in traffic." Crenshaw strode to the table with the confidence that he could have only been born out of years of dealing with men like Bayne. Her gaze hopped over each of the people at the table before landing on Logan. "Special Agent Elkins." She gave a tight-lipped smile. "Good to see you again."

Tracy Crenshaw had been a detective when he'd joined the force as a rookie. She looked as if she'd aged ten years since he'd last seen her, but he supposed that was a hazard of her job. Her hair was grayer than the red it had once been. She wore it in a bun, coiled tightly at the nape of her neck. Her suit was boxy, hiding any curves she might have had. A purposeful choice, Logan deduced. She didn't want the men she worked with to see her as a woman as much as a boss. He'd never worked with Crenshaw directly, but she had a reputation as a solid cop who put in the work. He was more than a little surprised that she knew of him, though.

He heard himself telling the lieutenant to please call him Logan, but his gaze was pinned over the lieutenant's shoulder at the woman who was obviously trying to look anywhere but directly at him.

"Let me introduce Detective Wendell Keene, on loan to us from the Third District until we catch this guy," Crenshaw said.

He didn't know if Keene had been on the force at the same time as he had, but the man's name and face weren't ringing any bells. Keene reached a hand across the table.

Logan felt himself taking the man's hand and shaking it, almost as if he was in a daze.

"And this is the lead detective on the case, Detective Dora Madison," Crenshaw continued.

Dora finally met his gaze head on. "Agent Elkins and I have met." Dora's expression gave nothing away. Was she happy to see him? Angry? Indifferent? There was a time when he could have read every thought she had and every emotion, but those days were long gone.

What he did know was that she was still a knockout. Her ebony skin glowed, and he wondered if it was as soft now as it had been two years ago. She'd allowed her dark brown hair to grow down below her shoulders in loose ringlets. She wore a dark pantsuit that accentuated her generous curves and low-heeled boots. And she still wore the freesia-scented perfume that drifted toward him and fired his blood.

Crenshaw looked from him to Dora. "You two worked together in the past?"

"Something like that," Dora said, her light brown eyes hard.

Dora marched past him to the conference room table, her tailored dark green suit hugging her slim figure. She was still as lovely as he'd ever seen her.

Dora held his gaze for a moment longer before looking away.

"Well then, let's get started." Chief Bayne waved the newcomers to the empty seats at the table and began the meeting.

Logan supposed he should be thankful that no one seemed to have noticed the tension between him and Dora.

"I've got a press conference scheduled in less than an hour," Bayne said, the statement sounding almost like a threat. "I need to let the city know we are on top of this. That we won't rest until we have this psychopath in custody. What do we have so far?"

Dora briefed the group on that morning's 911 call, the witness, and the results so far on the door-to-door canvass of the neighborhood.

"What can I take to the press?" Bayne said after Dora had been speaking for nearly ten minutes. "Did the witness give us a description of the perp? Do we have any solid evidence? DNA?"

Logan frowned. The 911 call about the body had only come in about eight hours earlier. Even if the cops had collected a DNA sample, Bayne had to know there was no way they'd have processed it yet. Even the FBI lab—one of the best in the world—couldn't have gotten results that quickly.

"We're still processing the evidence from the scene, sir," Dora responded. "The witness is…distraught. We spoke to her a little before she was transported to the hospital, where the doctors felt it was best to sedate her. Detective Keene and I are heading back to the hospital to speak to her after this meeting."

"Did the autopsy turn up anything useful?" Bayne pressed.

"It's scheduled for an hour from now."

"Her phone? The search of her house? The canvass?"

Keene stepped up to the plate this time. "Techs are working on unlocking the phone, sir. We have a team searching Ms. Quitoni's condo as we speak. The canvass is ongoing."

"So, I have to go out there and tell the press you have nothing." Bayne threw the pen he'd been tapping against the table down.

Jerk. The thought popped into Logan's mind unbidden. He pushed it aside and said, "Actually, Chief Bayne, I would suggest you hold off on telling the press anything at the moment."

Bayne's gaze whipped to him. "And why is that Special Agent Elkins? The public is rightly terrified that we have a serial killer stalking the streets of DC."

"You have a killer who is obviously seeking attention. He leaves his victims in public places where he knows they will be found. He also takes a considerable risk in being seen doing so. That tells me he craves an audience. That he might even seek a confrontation. If you go to the press now, you might give him exactly what he wants."

Bayne's eyes narrowed, his shoulders hunching forward. "And the people of this city? Am I just supposed to let them think the police don't care?"

You mean let them think you don't care? That wouldn't be good for whatever aspirations you have beyond being chief of police, now, would it?

"No, but I am saying that giving this killer what he's looking for will probably put the residents of this city in more danger, not less." Logan fought to keep his temper in check. It wouldn't do anyone any good to start off on the wrong foot. "If you feel you must speak to the press, simply assure them you are doing everything you can. Encourage anyone who may have been in the area of this third crime scene last night or this morning and saw something suspicious to come forward. Do the same for potential witnesses to the first two crimes and show photos of those victims. Hopefully, it will jog someone's memory."

"Do you really think it's wise to so explicitly connect the first two crimes to this one?" Deputy Mayor Carl Simone spoke up.

Of course the mayor's office would want to downplay the serial aspect of the case. It was bad for business. Tourists shied away from cities that had serial killers roaming the streets.

"The press is already connecting it for us," Dora chimed in, saving him from having to state the obvious. "Three women with the same exotic flower in their hair, a fact we'd been trying to keep out of the press. I'd love to know who leaked it," she added bitterly, "but the fact is, it's out there now."

The Metropolitan Police Department's press liaison cleared his throat. "My office has started getting questions about whether the department dropped the ball on the first two murders and whether we prioritize solving the murders of prominent victims over crimes against average citizens."

Bayne let out a string of curses. "Elkins, I can't go out there and just say some version of 'If you've seen something, say something.' The press would eat me alive."

"You can and you should," Logan shot back. "Isn't that what they pay you the big bucks for? To take the heat. If you go out there and goad this killer, the press could be the least of your worries."

Bayne glared across the table at him.

Logan held his gaze steady on the chief. He'd been brought in to do a job, and while he couldn't make Bayne take his professional advice, he wouldn't let the chief stop him from giving it.

"Can I just play devil's advocate here?" The deputy chief of police, Tina Linuesa, spoke up, her voice cutting through the tension in the room. "Is it possible that not giving the killer the attention he craves might anger him, thus driving him to commit even more murders?"

"It is possible," Logan conceded. "But he's already killed three women, and in killing Michelle Quitoni, he'll be getting more attention than he garnered after the first two murders, no matter what we do. I'm merely suggesting we don't throw gas on the fire."

Linuesa nodded in apparent agreement, but Bayne's frown didn't budge.

"Fine," Bayne growled after a minute of silence. "I'll keep the press conference brief and the details sparse. Madison, Keene, what did you get out of the witness?"

"Well, as I mentioned, she was very distressed," Dora started. "She was able to give us a general description of a Caucasian man, medium height, that she watched carry the body across the lawn."

"That's it? A white man of medium height. That could be anyone. Hell, that could be two of the people in this room," Bayne boomed, pointing from Carl Simone to one aide at the table. "Who is this woman? Why was she in the park so early in the morning?"

Keene and Dora shared a look.

"That's one thing we hope to ask her when we speak with her this afternoon. She would only give us her first name, Becky."

Bayne threw up his hands. "Great."

"There is something else you could speak about at your press conference, Chief," Tina Linuesa said, drawing all the eyes in the room to her. "Senator Quitoni has offered to post a two-hundred-fifty-thousand-dollar reward for anyone who has information leading to the arrest of his daughter's killer."

Logan hadn't spoken to Senator Quitoni, although he knew the senator had spoken to his boss and the director of the FBI briefly. Interviewing Michelle Quitoni's family and close friends was on his rapidly expanding to-do list.

He'd had enough experience with the parents of murder victims to know that they always wanted answers quickly, and given his prominent position and power, Logan knew the politician would be a thorn in his side until he got those answers. It was no surprise that Senator Quitoni had put up such a whopping reward. Powerful people thought money would bring all the answers. But in cases like the one they faced, a reward of that size was more likely to be a hindrance than a help.

"I'd advise against making the reward that big," Logan said.

"Of course you do," Bayne spat.

To Logan's surprise, Dora spoke up. "It will bring every crank and crook out of the woodwork. We'll get thousands of false leads, all of which we'll have to spend time and manpower running down."

Linuesa cocked her head to one side. "Maybe a more modest number, then?"

"Ten thousand," Logan said. "It's enough to catch the public's attention but not enough to have a con salivating."

Linuesa nodded. "I'll let Senator Quitoni know."

"Should the arrangements to take Senator Quitoni's statement be made through your office?" Keene asked Linuesa.

Logan noted the downturn in Dora's mouth. She didn't like that there would be a middleman between her and her victim's family, but it was an allowance regularly made for powerful or connected people, and a senator qualified as both.

"The senator passed along the contact information for his personal aide." Linuesa slid a business card from the leather portfolio in front of her onto the table. "You can call her to arrange to speak with the senator."

"I'd like to go with you when you conduct that interview, if you don't mind," Logan said.

Dora's mouth tugged down into a genuine frown now, but she nodded. "Of course."

"Take Special Agent Elkins with you when you interview the witness too," Lieutenant Crenshaw said. "It will be good to have his impressions of the woman if we are going to be relying on her description to catch our perp. The last thing we want to do is have the whole damn city on the lookout for the wrong man."

Bayne nodded. "Absolutely not. If she gives you enough for a composite sketch, get one, but don't release it without clearing it through my office first."

Crenshaw sat up straighter in her chair. "That's not our standard protocol."

"I don't care what standard protocol is. This case is too important to screw up. I'm the one that will be standing at that podium taking heat from the press, so I'm going to be riding herd on this one, Lieutenant. Understand?"

"Yes, sir," Crenshaw answered tightly.

"Good. Anything else?" Bayne asked, but he was already out of his seat. "We're adjourned."

Bayne strode from the room without a backward glance. Tina Linuesa and Carl Simone were only steps behind him.

Logan moved around the table and caught Dora's arm before she could exit the room.

"Dora. Got a moment?"

"Sure," she clipped, pulling her arm from his grasp.

"I just wanted to make sure our past isn't going to—"

"Our past," she said, cutting him off in a low voice while glancing around the room. Most of the meeting attendees had filed out of the room, but two of the chief's aides were conversing in low voices on the opposite side of the room. "Is just that. In the past. I have a job to do, and so do you."

He raised his hands. "I didn't mean to upset you."

"You haven't upset me," she said, her voice rising enough to draw a glance from one aide. She blew out a deep breath. "You haven't upset me," she repeated more quietly. "I would simply prefer it if we kept our discussion strictly in the professional realm from this point forward. I think it's best."

Dora didn't meet his gaze. He couldn't say he didn't deserve her anger.

They'd met right after he'd applied to the FBI. He'd fully expected the relationship to go the way most of his relationships had prior to that. They'd spend a few great weeks together, maybe a month or two, and then things would start to peter out. Or in some cases, explode in a fiery mess that usually ended with lots of name calling and door slamming. Either way, he hadn't expected to spend nine pretty great months with Dora. To be honest, he'd been thinking about the future, their future—but then he'd gotten the call to interview with the FBI.

Things had moved fast after that. Joining the Bureau had been a dream of his since he'd decided on a career in law enforcement, but he hadn't told anyone other than his brother, Landon. He hadn't mentioned it to Dora at all. What it had come down to was that he'd felt he'd had to choose between his career and Dora. Nine months might have been a long time for him to have a relationship, but it wasn't long enough to expect her to put her life on hold for him. So, he'd taken the job, broken up with Dora, and headed out to his new duty station in Arizona.

It had not taken long before he realized what he'd left behind. As much as he loved the job and the Bureau, and he did, he'd missed Dora. And the longing for her hadn't dissipated at all as first one year and then another had passed.

He'd considered calling her when he'd gotten word that he was being transferred back to Washington, DC, but frankly, he'd been too ashamed of how he'd left. He'd convinced himself that she'd moved on with her life, had gotten over him, and that he needed to do the same. He'd even been proud of himself for not googling her like some lovesick teenager.

But fate had other plans. Now that he'd seen her and was going to be working side by side with her, he knew that what he wanted most in the world was another chance. He just hoped she wanted the same thing.

"Whatever you think is best," he responded through clenched teeth.

"Good." She glanced at her watch. "I want to see if the medical examiner has anything for me yet. Would you like to go with me?"

It was rare for him to attend an autopsy. Usually, he had to rely upon the medical examiner's report, but viewing the victim could give him some insight into the killer's mind and certainly his signature.

He nodded. "Yes."

"Fine, then." Dora returned his nod. "Let's go."

Chapter Four

Dora skimmed emails and dodged pedestrians on the short walk from the station to the medical examiner's office. Anything to avoid making small talk with Logan. Why couldn't he have grown a beer belly and receding hairline in the last two years? How did he manage to get even more handsome—heck, she'd say it but only to herself—sexy? Broad shoulders, tapered hips, and lips that were made for kissing.

Don't think about kissing!

She stole a glance at Logan. He'd buttoned his coat up to his neck, but it was an unusually warm January day. A thin sheen of perspiration had begun blooming on the brown skin on his forehead.

The man looks good even when he's sweating. She heard the words in her mother's voice, and a ping of yearning shot through her. She missed her mother, but after raising a child all on her own, Pearl Madison deserved to live her life for herself. Dora just wished her mother had found happiness in Washington, DC, or at least on the East Coast. Five years ago, her mother had gone on a cruise and met Felix Mayberry. The two had fallen for each other fast and, just four months after meeting, had gotten married. Despite the speed of their courtship, Dora thought Felix was a great guy and a great guy for her mother. His one flaw was that he lived in San Francisco. Her mother had decided if she was going to go on the adventure, she was going to go all the way and had moved across the country.

Dora made a mental note to call her mother. She was sure Pearl had some words of wisdom that would help settle the emotions churning inside Dora at the moment.

They arrived at the medical examiner's office and signed in before heading to the basement, where the autopsies were done. She and Logan slid their arms through thin protective gowns and snapped booties over their shoes before pushing through the heavy swinging doors that led into the medical examiner's lab.

Dean Schroff, the medical examiner, looked up from the victim he'd been examining on the table as they entered, his clear blue eyes landing on Dora. Dean was one of the youngest medical examiners at thirty-two, but he was also one of the best. He shook his curly, dirty blond hair out of his eyes and said, "I'm not finished my exam." He turned back to the body on the table.

Dora snagged the tube of menthol from Dean's desk. She dabbed a bit under her nose before passing the tube to Logan, who did the same. "I'll take whatever you have so far."

"Who's he?" Dean asked. Dean had only taken the job of head medical examiner for the District of Columbia a year earlier, right after Logan had gone over to the FBI, so their paths would not have crossed before.

"Logan Elkins. I'm former MPD and currently a profiler with the FBI here to help Detective Madison on this case."

Dean glanced up again, studying Logan for a long moment.

"Dean," Dora said when Dean's inspection had gone

on long enough to be awkward, "have you got anything for me or not?"

Dean slowly slid his gaze from Logan to Dora. "I told you I'm not finished—"

Dora opened her mouth to protest, but Dean stopped her.

"But I have found some interesting details." Dean moved from the head of the steel table to the midpoint. "The victim wasn't beaten or sexually assaulted. There's some bruising, but that is probably from the victim struggling against restraints."

"So just like the other victims," Logan said. "He doesn't hurt them physically if he can help it."

Dean gave a nod. "I found this tangled in the victim's hair."

Dean held the jar out to Dora. She took it and held it up so Logan could examine the contents at the same time she did.

"It's a flower," Logan said.

"The exotic and not easily found in Washington, DC, desert rose, to be exact," Dean repeated. "Just like with the first and second victims found tangled in the hair."

"We've kept that quiet," Dora said at Logan's confused expression. "We don't want the media to get wind of it."

Logan nodded his understanding. "Something to weed out the fake reports."

"Exactly," Dora responded. "Both victims were found in the park, and the second victim was found in a field overrun with the stuff."

"Do you think a third victim with it in their hair will finally get the brass to use the dreaded term *serial killer*?" Dean questioned.

She had her doubts. "I don't know."

"There's one other thing I want to show you," Dean said.

He rolled the victim onto her side so that Dora and Logan could see the words written on her back. The killer had written on the victim: *Protect the innocent*.

Dora made no attempt to hide her fury and disgust. From the look on their faces, Dean and Logan felt similarly. "I really want to catch this guy."

"And I really hope you do." Dean lowered the body onto her back once again. "And quickly," he added pointedly.

Dora didn't need to ask why. A killer with this much rage...wouldn't stop until they were stopped.

TRUE TO FORM, Crenshaw barely let Dora get to her desk before calling for an update on the case. Dora motioned for Logan, who had somehow managed to secure himself the empty desk facing her own, to follow her. When they arrived at the lieutenant's office, they found the small space already bursting at the seams. The lieutenant's office was designed like a fishbowl, with glass walls running along three sides. However, Crenshaw's organizational skills left much to be desired. Five-drawer vertical file cabinets ran the length of one wall, blocking most of the view of the right side of the bullpen. A low credenza stacked high with files, notebooks, and other papers occupied the other side of the office allowing a slightly less obstructed view of the left side of the bullpen, but only slightly. Crenshaw sat behind her desk. Keene sat in one of the visitor's chairs facing the lieutenant, while Detective Bill Roberts leaned against a tall file cabinet, a steaming mug in his hands.

Roberts was nearing his twenty years and, rumor had it, on the way out. Dora had worked with him on two or three cases over the years and hadn't been impressed. He wasn't a bad cop, but he tended to miss details and to go into situations with preconceived notions. She held in a sigh. She'd have to be careful how she used him on this case. She couldn't afford mistakes or setbacks.

"Madison, Elkins, come in." Lieutenant Crenshaw waved them into the office as if there was plenty of space for two more bodies.

Logan nodded to the second unoccupied chair in the room, but Dora gave a slight shake of her head. She preferred to stand when she was making her reports.

Logan gave a small shrug and sat.

"Elkins, the big guy behind you with a mug of green tea is Detective Roberts. I'm assigning him to the case along with you, Dora, and Keene. I have every confidence that with my best detectives and an FBI profiler we can get this case solved ASAP." Crenshaw glared from across her desk. "Okay, so where are we?" Crenshaw asked with a hint of irritation in her tone.

Dora felt a matching flicker of irritation rumble in her own chest. They'd discovered their most recent victim less than six hours earlier, and Logan still needed to get up to speed. They were nowhere, the same as they'd been for weeks now.

But she couldn't say that to the lieutenant, so instead she said, "Logan and I were just with Dean." She ran through what the Dean had told them about the manner of death being strangulation and his official determination of homicide.

Keene whispered a low curse, but Crenshaw didn't bother to whisper.

"Damn it." The lieutenant slapped her palm against her desk, then swung her eyes to Logan. "That's three. So, we've officially got a serial killer, right?"

"Well, it's not that easy," Logan answered, before

quickly adding, "but I am inclined to think that the same person killed all three of your victims, yes."

"'Inclined to think.'" Crenshaw shot the words like daggers back at Logan. "Okay, tell us why you are *inclined to think* that."

"You have three victims—Monica Gonzalez, Alicia Jones, and Michelle Quitoni. All between the ages of twenty-five and thirty-five, and all brunettes. None were what we'd consider high risk. Based on the reports forwarded to me, none of our victims had ever been involved in drugs or gambling. No one had ever reported an abusive husband or boyfriend. No issues at work. Monica was a cashier, Alicia was a preschool teacher, and Michelle was an investment banker. Nothing in any of their backgrounds that we've discovered so far would suggest they'd meet the end they did."

"And yet they did."

"Yes, but that tells us something. These women may not have been at high risk, but each of them crossed paths with the killer at some point."

"I have only been on the case for an hour, so I'm still catching up," Roberts spoke up from his perch against the filing cabinets, "but I did skim Dora's interim reports on the first two victims. She hadn't found anything that suggested the victims knew each other."

Logan turned in his chair so that he was looking at Roberts when he answered. "They didn't have to know each other. Their paths just had to cross each other, and not even at the same time. They might not have even been aware of it."

Dora nodded, catching on to the thread of Logan's thoughts. "Like they both could use the same grocery store or beautician. They might not know they patronize the same place, but our killer does."

Logan shifted again, his gaze falling on her, and smiled. Her heart fluttered.

"Exactly," he said, holding her gaze for one moment longer before turning back around to face Crenshaw.

The lieutenant was not smiling. "Then how exactly do we find this guy?"

"We need to learn as much as we can about each of the victim's daily habits. Where they shopped, where they went for lunch, their favorite coffee shop—everything. And we need to know if there had been any changes in their habits lately. Even something small or innocuous like changing dry cleaners might have put them in the path of our unsub."

Keene groaned. "Do you know how many man hours compiling that kind of information for three people will eat up?"

Logan patted the younger detective on the back. "Sorry, but profiling is not like they make it out on television. It is mostly collecting and shifting through mounds of data until I can paint a vivid enough picture to see the unsub."

"There was one other piece of information we got from Dean that might help with painting that picture," Dora offered.

Lieutenant Crenshaw arched her brow.

"The killer wrote a message on Michelle Quitoni."

"He wrote on her?" Keene said, his eyes wide with shock.

His surprise reminded Dora just how green the detective was. She nodded. "Yes."

"What did he write?" Roberts asked in a wary tone. He'd been on the force the longest of all of them, even longer than Crenshaw. Dora wouldn't be surprised if nothing shocked him. She had once overheard one of the other detectives ask Roberts why he hadn't tried to rise higher in the ranks. Roberts had responded with a detailed cost benefit analysis which had amounted to *it wasn't worth the headache*. At the time, she'd marked Roberts as lacking ambition, but the longer she was in the job the more she understood where he was coming from. She was no longer sure she wanted to become one of the brass, pushing paper and worried about politics day in and day out. Doing the real work of putting the bad guys away meant being in the trenches.

"Dora?" Crenshaw barked.

Dora jerked out of her thoughts. "Sorry. He wrote 'Protect the innocent,'" Dora added.

"This sicko has got some messed-up definition of protecting the innocent," Keene spat.

"Maybe, maybe not," Logan said. "The question is whether the killer sees these women as innocent or not. If he thinks they are innocent, he may also think that by killing them he is protecting them."

Dora felt her mouth turn down in a frown. "And if he doesn't think his victims are innocent?"

Logan turned in his chair, looking at her again. "He may feel as if, by killing them, he *is* protecting the innocent."

"So, either way he's delusional," Roberts offered.

Logan shrugged facing forward again. "Serial killers aren't known for their rational behavior, Detective."

"All right," Crenshaw said, running her hands through her already messy hair and leaning back in her chair. "Whatever his reason, motivations, or mental state, we need to find this guy, like yesterday. Have you talked to our witness again?"

Dora stood up straighter. "That's my next stop."

"Good." The lieutenant swept her gaze over each of them in turn. "The four of you go do whatever you have to do to get this guy off the street."

Chapter Five

Their witness, Randi Singer, was seventeen and homeless, which Logan knew created an additional layer of problems for any investigation, not the least of which was finding stable housing for the duration of the investigation. Dora had successfully found Randi a bed at Sunset House, a halfway house for women and children in need.

Sunset House turned out to be a large colonial in an older modest neighborhood. The street was quiet, and trees lined it. There was nothing at all to indicate that the home served as a refuge, which was the point. Hiding in plain sight, so to speak.

Dora had called before they'd left the police station to let Randi and Violet Fullerton, the halfway house Dora had found for Randi, know they were coming. Violet Fullerton answered the door and led them down a short hallway. Randi was waiting for them in the living room, which had obviously been furnished with hand-me-down furniture but also included a large flat-screen television that was mounted to the wall over a stone fireplace. Randi still looked much older than her seventeen years, but she at least looked rested now. Violet had gotten her some clean clothes, and it looked as if she'd gotten her hair washed and trimmed.

"Randi, hi," Dora said, entering the room and pulling her badge out of her jacket pocket. "I don't know if you remember me, but I'm Detective Dora Madison."

Randi chewed the nail on her index finger. "I remember you." Her gaze shifted to Logan.

"And I'm Logan Elkins. I'm working on the case with Detective Madison."

Randi cocked her head to the side. "Are you her partner?"

Logan slid a look at Dora.

"No," Dora answered quickly. "Special Agent Elkins is with the FBI."

Randi's head tilted even farther, but she didn't offer a response.

Dora took a seat perched in the easy chair opposite the sofa. Logan sat in the armchair to her right.

"Randi, we know you've been through a lot. We were hoping that you could answer a few questions for us, though. Would that be okay?"

"More questions," Randi whined, reminding Logan that the girl was a mere seventeen years old. She was only a year older than his own niece.

"It would be really helpful," Logan offered gently. "We really need to catch this guy before he hurts someone else."

Randi hesitated for a moment longer before giving a faint nod.

"Thank you." Dora took a small notebook from her jacket pocket and uncapped a pen.

He preferred a more hands-free approach. "Randi, do you mind if I record the conversation? Just to make it easier for me to remember things later. I won't share the recording with anyone not investigating the case."

Randi nodded. "Sure, yeah, whatever."

Logan hit the Record button on his cell phone and waited. Dora was the lead investigator. It was her show.

"Let's start with something easy," Dora said. "Where are you from?"

Randi brought her index finger to her mouth again. "Lots of places. My father moved us around a lot before he died."

"When did your father pass away?" Logan asked.

"Two years ago." She ducked her head, trying to hide the shimmer of tears, but he'd seen it. So, she wasn't a runaway but a kid who had suffered a hard knock early in life and was finding it hard to recover on her own.

"What about your mother?"

Randi shrugged. "Don't know her. Dad said she abandoned us when I was too young to remember."

Dora scribbled a note on her pad. "Do you know her name? Where she lives? Maybe we can contact her for you."

"No." The single word left no room for negotiation. Randi was seventeen, almost an adult legally. If she didn't want her mother in her life, there was nothing Dora or anyone else could do to force her.

"Okay. Could you tell us why you were in the park last night?"

Randi's eyes narrowed with suspicion. "What does that matter?"

Logan cleared his throat. "It helps us understand the circumstances surrounding the night—that's all."

Randi was quiet for a beat more before she spoke again. "I was just hanging out."

That could mean a whole host of things—drugs, alcohol, meeting a john—the one thing it most likely didn't include was simply chatting with friends.

He shot another look at Dora, but she remained focused on her witness.

"Okay," Dora said, scratching another note on the page in front of her. "Could you tell us what you saw?"

Randi shifted on the sofa, her knee bouncing in time to some unheard music. "I already told you everything I know."

"I know we spoke yesterday." Dora kept her voice low and gentle, but Logan could hear the edge of annoyance in her tone.

No doubt Randi did too. Her knee bounced faster.

He slid forward in his chair and clasped his hands in front of him. "Sometimes a good night's rest helps us to recall little details we don't think about in the initial moments after an event." He smiled encouragingly at the young woman across from him. "Anything you can tell us now will be so helpful, Randi."

He watched as Randi's body visibly relaxed. He'd been told he had a way with interviews. It was part of what made him a good profiler. He was excellent at reading people. And what he read when he looked at Randi was that she was a scared young woman who'd been through more than her fair share of crap in her short life. It wasn't fair that they were asking even more of her now, but it was necessary if they wanted to catch a killer.

"I was hanging out in the park just walking around—"

"Was anyone with you?" Dora interrupted.

Randi shook her head. "No. I'm kind of a loner. Safer that way."

Logan wasn't sure that was true at all, but it wasn't worth mentioning it now.

"I saw a man and a woman. At least I thought it was a woman. They were on the ground. I thought they were..."

Randi's face flushed. "You know. I was about to turn away, but something seemed...off."

"Off? Off how?" Logan interrupted this time.

Randi's face scrunched up, her gaze going up and to the left as if she was trying to grasp onto the words to answer his question but couldn't quite catch them. "I'm not sure. Just off."

"That's okay," Dora said. "Sometimes 'off' is just our subconscious telling us to be careful."

"I guess." Randi's finger went back to her mouth. "I just knew that I shouldn't let the man know that I was there, you know? I hid behind this big tree and watched him."

"What did he do?" Dora had scooted to the edge of the easy chair now as well.

"He was petting her." Randi shivered at the memory. "Like smoothing her clothes and making sure she looked okay, I think. He tucked something into her hair, and then he kissed her on the lips and walked away toward the parking lot."

She swallowed hard. "That's when I realized this wasn't some freaky date night. The woman didn't get up and go with him. She didn't move at all. I wasn't sure if I should go over to her—like, if she might yell at me or whatever—but she was so still. I thought she might need help."

"You did exactly the right thing," Logan said.

Randi's eyes locked onto him. He could see the fear she must have felt in those moments reflected in her eyes now. "I knew she was dead when I got a good look at her, so I ran."

"To the convenience store?" Dora said softly.

Randi's head bobbed up and down. "Yeah. The night manager there lets me use the ladies' room even though he's not supposed to unlock the door for anyone after ten.

He let me in, and he called the cops when I told him what I saw."

He'd read the responding officer's report. The convenience store manager hadn't provided anything helpful. He'd called the cops when Randi arrived, and they'd both waited at the store for help.

"Can you remember anything else?" Dora asked now. "Any sounds? Smells? See anyone else at all?"

Randi's gaze fell to the floor. "No."

There was something there. Something she didn't want to say.

Logan glanced at Dora again. This time she met his gaze, the look on her face indicating that she was thinking exactly what he was.

"Would you be willing to work with a sketch artist, Randi?"

"I... I don't know. I already told you. It was dark. The guy was white, kind of tall, but other than that I didn't see anything."

Somewhere in the house a door slammed. Randi startled, her eyes darting around the room.

Logan gave her a moment to settle before he said, "You'd be surprised what a sketch artist can pull from your memory. Why don't you give it a try? I'm sure Detective Madison will even spring for lunch afterward."

Dora's smile was tight enough that he knew he'd pay for the suggestion later. "Sure. What do you say, Randi?"

"I guess. At least I'll have something to do. How long am I going to have to stay at this place?"

"Do you have someplace else you can go?" Logan asked gently.

Randi didn't answer, which was an answer in itself.

"I've arranged for you to stay here for the time being.

I'm sure that Violet could use some help around here. There's always something that needs doing."

Randi scratched her elbow. "Yeah, maybe."

Dora's smile this time was genuine, and it hit him like a punch to the gut. He'd forgotten how beautiful she was when she smiled.

Now is not the time.

"Great," Dora said rising. Logan followed suit. "I'll pick you up tomorrow at ten. You decide where you'd like to have lunch."

For the first time since they'd entered Sunset House, Randi smiled. "Anywhere?"

Dora let out a small groan, but the smile remained on her lips. "Anywhere that is manageable by a cop's salary."

"Oh." Randi turned to Logan. "I bet FBI agents make more than DC cops." Her brows rose.

"Oh, they definitely do." Dora clapped a hand on Logan's shoulder. "And I know Special Agent Elkins wouldn't miss lunch with you for the world."

Dora turned her smile on him directly, and there wasn't much he wouldn't have promised to keep it there. "Sure. Lunch is on me tomorrow. Anywhere you want, Randi."

Chapter Six

Dora drove to a nearby family-owned Chinese restaurant that served an amazing dim sum. The interior of the restaurant was warm and welcoming. She and Logan followed the hostess to a table.

Dora was a regular and didn't need to look at the menu before ordering. Logan placed an order for dumplings and sweet-and-sour pork, and they both got oolong tea.

"So how long have you been back in town?" Dora asked, jumping right in. If they were going to be working together, she wanted to get the awkward questions out of the way.

"Not long. A couple of months." Logan held her gaze. "I wanted to call you, but I didn't know if I should."

She didn't respond. Mostly because she didn't know how she would have reacted if he had called. Instead, she cleared her throat and changed the subject.

"How are Lisa and Landon? Is Landon still catching the bad guys and Lisa still fighting cybercrime?" she asked, keeping her tone light. Landon, his older brother and an investigative reporter, seemed to be more open-minded about his sister's role in the justice system.

"They're both good, work wise at least. Layla is sixteen, and she and Lisa are butting heads more often now."

Dora had trouble imagining Logan's niece, a pretty, shy

young girl the last time Dora had seen her, pushing back against her mother, but she had heard that the teen years could be hard on mothers and daughters.

"Wow. Sixteen. Time flies."

"That it does," Logan concurred. "Layla seems to have made it through her parent's divorce relatively unscathed."

"I remember Lisa and Charles's marriage was on rocky ground when..." *When we'd been together*, but instead of saying the words she let the rest of the statement trail off.

Logan gave her a look. "Yeah, they decided to call it quits. It was rough for everyone, but they seem to have found a system that works for them. Charles and Lisa were never a good fit for each other, but they both unequivocally love Layla more than anything else. They've been committed to getting her through this period with as little trauma as possible. They're good parents."

"That's good." Dora swallowed and reached for her water. Something about the conversation was feeling a little too intimate, too much like a conversation between two people in a personal relationship. But that was not what they were. They were colleagues and colleagues only. It looked like she was going to have to remind herself of that often while they were working together.

She searched her brain for another topic of conversation. Her gaze landed on the plates on the table in front of them.

Dora chuckled. "I'm sure I'd forgotten how much you eat."

"Fast metabolism." Logan dug into his food. "I remember that you'll work until you drop."

Their server, the owner's grandson, brought out their orders.

"You sure you don't need more to eat?" Logan asked, eyeing her single plate before glancing back at his multiple dishes, I seem to remember you forgetting to eat more than once."

"I eat when necessary." Dora speared a pork dumpling. She chewed, ignoring Logan's skeptical look. "What do you think of the case so far?" she asked, changing the subject once again.

"We're still early."

"I know, but I'm just wondering what you're thinking. Are we headed in the right direction? Is there any way to narrow down the pool of suspects?"

Logan sighed. "Dora, I can't just wave a magic wand. Profiling isn't an exact science. The more evidence we gather, the more I'll be able to refine the profile of our killer, but I'll never be able to give you a name and address. Only good old-fashioned police work will get you that."

Dora scowled. "More evidence likely means another woman will be killed. I want to avoid that."

Logan lowered his chopsticks. "I do too, but one thing I've had to come to terms with in this job is that, more often than not, I'll be too late to save the victim. The only thing I can do is use my skills to potentially save the next one."

"What if I don't think that's good enough?"

"It has to be," Logan shot back. "You know that. If you let yourself get consumed with the ones you couldn't save, you'll drive yourself mad."

Dora's scowl only deepened. She knew he was right, but that didn't stop her from feeling responsible. She was supposed to catch the bad guys, and so far, it was bad guy three, Dora zero. She pushed her half-eaten lunch to the side. "We should get back to work."

Logan sighed again and wiped his hands on his napkin.

Dora got the waiter's attention, signaling that they were

ready for the check. The server quickly brought over the bill, handing it to Logan even though she had called for it.

She stretched her hand across the table, but Logan snatched the bill before she could reach it.

Her scowl deepened. "What's my part come to?"

He took several bills out of his wallet and placed them inside the folder. "Don't worry about it. My treat."

Dora sat up straighter in her chair. "That's nice of you," she said deservedly, "but I like to pay my own way."

Logan rolled his eyes. "Your part came to next to nothing compared to mine, and I was the one who insisted on stopping to eat. Let me get this."

Dora started to argue again.

"Dora, I got this. You can get the next one, okay?"

She wasn't happy about it, but it wasn't worth arguing about any further. Not when they had work to do. "Okay," she responded grudgingly. After another beat, she added, "Thank you."

"You're welcome," Logan replied as they rose and headed to the car. "Now, where to next?"

WHEN LOGAN TRIED to arrange a meeting with Senator Quitoni and his wife, he'd been told that the senator and Mrs. Quitoni were too distraught. He was told to call the next day to see if the senator was feeling strong enough to speak to them.

Logan was frustrated by the senator putting them off. He'd have thought that Michelle's parents would want to do everything they could to find their daughter's killer. But he understood that diplomacy would be needed here. The senator was powerful, and powerful people often had to be treated with kid gloves. He'd call tomorrow, but if the senator "wasn't up for speaking to them" then, he'd have a talk with Lieutenant Crenshaw and his own bosses.

He and Dora spent the rest of the day reviewing the reports from the witness canvasses, attempting to identify anyone who saw something that would warrant a second interview and trying to nail down Michelle's movements over her last days. It was the tedious, unsexy work that often led to a suspect but never made it onto the television and movie screens. It was the kind of work that showed the mettle of a good cop, and Dora was a good cop. Methodical, thoughtful, and attentive to the smallest details. When he finally knocked off for the night, Dora was still at her desk.

His older brother, Landon, had sent a text earlier that afternoon asking if Logan could stop by when he had a chance. Logan was still too wired to go home, so he pointed his car in another familiar direction. His parents had bought their Brightwood Park home more than forty years earlier. A short walk away from the Fort Totten metro station, it was a sleepy neighborhood filled with families. When they'd purchased the home, they couldn't have imagined how much it would appreciate over the succeeding four decades.

He found a parking space at the end of the street and walked back to the house, using his key to let himself in. Logan stuffed his gloves and hat into the pocket of his coat and tossed the coat over the arm of the sofa. He made his way past boxes of flooring into the kitchen.

"The remodel is coming along," Logan said by way of greeting his older brother. Landon flashed a quick smile from his seat at the kitchen table. He'd been focused on something on his laptop screen. Landon had taken after their father and become an investigative reporter.

"It's getting there," his brother said.

The footprint of the kitchen would always be small—that was the way it was with row houses. But the space now boasted brand-new top-of-the-line appliances and sparkling white granite countertops.

"Still getting it all together," Landon said, pointing to the upper cabinets which waited to be hung on the floor against the kitchen wall.

Logan wrapped a bottle of water from the fridge and took a long swig, sitting at the table next to his brother. "I'd help you put them up, but I just caught a case that's going to tie up most of my time for a while."

"Don't worry about it." Landon closed the laptop. "I can handle it myself."

"Yeah, but you shouldn't have to," Logan said, feeling guilty not for the first time.

All three of the siblings had inherited the home after their mother's death. Landon had taken responsibility for it since Lisa owned her own place and Logan had moved to Arizona. Landon's plan was to renovate the house, which they'd all agreed to since their mother hadn't so much as painted since the early nineties. Once the work was done, they hoped to sell the place for a good sum. College-fund money, as Lisa had labeled it.

Landon reached over and clasped Logan on the shoulder. "Listen, don't worry about it. I got it."

Logan nodded, but the guilt was still there.

"I'm glad you could make it over tonight," Landon said. "Your text made it seem important."

Landon stood. "I think it could be. I found something."

Logan followed Landon back into the living room.

Landon sat on the sofa and pulled a strongbox that

Logan had passed unnoticed when he entered the house across the coffee table. Logan sat next to his brother.

"I found this in the attic."

"What were you doing in the attic?" Logan asked.

"It's a good space. You can stand up there—in most spots at least. I thought it might make a good office or spare room."

It had been years since Logan had ventured into his mother's attic. The thing he remembered most about it was the cobwebs and how creepy it felt to him. But if Logan said it was usable and, more importantly, valuable space, Logan didn't doubt him.

"So, what is this?" Logan asked, turning the conversation back to the strongbox in front of them.

Landon opened the box. Inside was an old notebook, and beside it was a handgun.

Logan leaned forward to look at the contents more closely but didn't touch them. "Where did you find this exactly?"

"In a crawl space in the attic. I'm not sure I ever knew it existed before today, but when I moved some of the boxes Mom had stashed up there the cover to the crawl-space fell off."

The layer of dust that covered the contents had been disturbed.

"You check the gun?"

Landon nodded. "Unloaded."

"I'm not sure why you are showing this to me," Logan said again.

"I think this stuff belongs to Dad. In fact, I'm sure of it. The writing in the notebook is definitely his."

Landon had been fifteen, Logan thirteen, when their father was murdered. They were old enough to have lasting memories of their father, including being able to identify his handwriting on sight.

Logan reached for the notebook and flipped it open. Most of the text was indecipherable, written in some sort of code, but Landon was right. The handwriting was that of their father's.

"You think the gun was Dad's too?" Logan queried.

"Seems that way. It makes sense. I know he'd been threatened once or twice over a story. I heard him and Mom arguing about it when I was younger."

Logan hadn't known that, but he knew his father had been a dogged reporter who had taken on some powerful people in Washington, DC, from time to time to get a story. Samuel Elkins's mantra had been to "speak truth to power." Logan knew from experience that "power" didn't always appreciate hearing the truth.

"Okay, I'm still not sure why you're showing me all this," Logan said.

"Look here," Landon said, pointing to the only two words on the page that didn't appear to have been written in code. "There are names—William Burgess and Addison Kober."

Logan looked up at the ceiling, thinking. "Burgess. Burgess."

"William Burgess is the Australian ambassador, though he wasn't when Dad would have written this."

"If this note refers to the same man. You have no way of knowing that," Logan pointed out.

"But it's possible, and that's enough reason for me to check it out. Especially when I factor in Addison Kober."

That was a name he knew. Addison Kober had disappeared shortly before their father's death. She'd been fifteen, the same age as Landon at the time, and her disappearance had been all over the Washington, DC, media for weeks.

"Why would he hide this? I mean, I get why he'd stash the gun with us kids in the house. But what about the journal?" Landon said.

"I...don't know. We may never know."

Their father had been dead for twenty years, and their mother, who might have been able to answer these questions for them, had been dead for two years now. Time had dulled the pain of their father's loss, but just the memory of his mother, Carolyn, was still strong enough to send a bolt of grief through Logan strong enough to snatch his breath away.

It was a moment before his lungs began to function again.

"I think these notes—" Landon held up the journal, seemingly unaware of Logan's swirling emotions "—might help us figure out what Dad was working on when he was killed. And maybe who could have killed him."

Logan sighed. He knew that Landon had been carrying on his own side investigation into their father's murder for years. Hell, he wasn't ashamed to admit that he had pulled some strings himself when he'd worked for the MPD and looked at the report on the investigation, such that it was. The file had been sparse on facts, witnesses, and evidence.

His father's body had been found in an alleyway with several stab wounds. One witness, a woman living in an adjacent apartment building, had thought she might have heard yelling, but she didn't see anyone or recognize the voices. The cops confirmed that Samuel had been at his favorite bar, O'Sullivan's, earlier that night. There hadn't been anything out of the ordinary, according to the regular bartender. Around midnight, his father had received a call on his cell phone. He closed his tab and left soon after. The bartender had not known who the call came from, and if the cops had looked into it any further, that information hadn't found its way into the file. Their father's cell phone, watch, and wallet were missing when his body was found. General consensus was that the murder had been a random robbery homicide, and the case had gone cold.

Landon had never bought that explanation, and Logan wasn't sure he did either. But he wasn't going to let the unanswered questions consume his life. Not like his father's stories had consumed him. And not like their father's unsolved murder appeared to be slowly consuming Landon's life.

"Look, Lan, I know it's hard to make peace with the fact that we may never have answers about Dad's death—"

"Murder," Landon interrupted, his voice hard. "Dad was murdered. And we could have answers if anyone bothered to look."

Logan held his hands out. "I don't want to argue with you. I'm just saying cold cases aren't as easy to solve as the television shows make it seem."

"I'm an investigative reporter." Landon glared. "Don't you think I know that?"

Logan wasn't sure, but he knew he'd do whatever he could to help his brother. "What do you want for me?"

"Do you think you could get me a copy of the MPD file on Dad's murder?"

"Landon—"

"I know it's a big ask, but—"

"It's a huge ask. I don't have direct access to the MPD's system anymore. And even when I did, there was a firewall between me and all the information on Dad's case."

"But you're working with the MPD now, right? Couldn't you ask Dora—"

Logan shot his brother a look. "Don't go there."

"Look, I wouldn't ask if it wasn't important. No one else cares about finding his killer anymore, if they ever did. I'm all that he has if he's going to get any justice."

"You're not all he has," Logan growled, standing.

Landon had the decency to look embarrassed. "I didn't mean it like that. It's just... Maybe you're right. Maybe I'm a little obsessed, but I can't let it go. Not without doing everything I can to find his killer. You understand that, right?"

Because he did understand, most of Logan's ire toward his brother faded away. "No promises," Logan said, grabbing his coat and heading for the front door. "I'll see what I can do."

Chapter Seven

Logan was happy to discover a text letting him know that Senator Quitoni and his wife were ready to speak to him. The Senator had insisted that the "conversation," as his people had termed it, be held at the Senator's residence. Since he firmly believed beggars couldn't be choosers, he met Dora at the police station, and they drove to the Senator's house together.

Senator Preston Quitoni lived on a sprawling estate in Great Falls, about thirty-five minutes from Capitol Hill. A tall iron fence ran around the tree-spotted property. The red-brick colonial sat two full football fields back from the street.

Dora swung the unmarked police sedan past the multiple news vans parked at the curb along the street from the corner and down past the senator's property. Cameras had been set up alongside the vans on the sidewalk. A half dozen reporters milled about on their phones, chatting, waiting for something to happen. They looked up as the car rolled by. The two bravest made their way toward the driveway, but two very large men materialized out of a gatehouse that blended into the line of cedar trees so well that Dora hadn't even noticed it at first.

"I bet the neighbors are loving this," Logan deadpanned.

Dora snorted. "I'm sure the local precinct is getting an earful, but it's a public street, so..." She shrugged and turned the sedan into the driveway, stopping beside an intercom.

A voice crackled from the speaker. "May I help you?"

"Detective Dora Madison from the Washington, DC, Metropolitan Police Department and Special Agent Logan Elkins of the FBI here to speak with Senator and Mrs. Quitoni."

The intercom crackled again. "Please hold your credentials up to the camera."

They did as requested, and after a moment, the disembodied voice said, "Very well."

The intercom clicked off, and the gates in front of them opened.

A young woman in black slacks and a white apron answered the door. Dora and Logan stepped into a large foyer with honey-brown teak flooring, wood-paneled walls, and an elaborate chandelier hanging overhead.

The maid led them to a sitting room larger than Dora's entire apartment. She recognized the man and woman sitting on the sofa as Senator and Mrs. Quitoni. The other man in the room she didn't know, but she didn't need to know his name to know that he was a lawyer. The thousand-dollar suit and constipated expression were dead giveaways.

The suit stepped forward, extending his hand. "Detectives, I am Cory Mase, of Mase, Black, and Glass. I'm the Quitonis' personal attorney."

Dora shook Mase's hand. "I'm the detective." She hooked her thumb at Logan. "He's a special agent with the FBI."

"Yes, of course, my apologies. Special Agent Elkins, is it?"

Logan gave Mase's hand a cursory shake. "Yes."

"Special Agent, Detective, my clients have been through an extraordinary loss. I've advised them to take more time to grieve before speaking to you, but the senator has insisted on doing whatever it takes to help you find the monster who did this to his daughter."

"Well, we appreciate that," Logan said. "The more information we can get, the better chance we will have at catching your daughter's killer," Dora said.

"Of course. I just ask that you respect the Quitonis' precarious emotional state at the moment."

Dora nodded noncommittally. The law might treat every person the same in theory, but in practice she was sitting in front of a man with vast power.

Mase stepped back beside the sofa his clients were sitting on. Dora sank into an armchair across from the sofa, and Logan took the matching chair beside her. A coffee table in a rich, dark mahogany separated the armchairs and sofa.

"First, please let me extend condolences on behalf of myself and the Metropolitan Police Department," Dora started.

"Thank you, Detective," Mrs. Quitoni replied.

The maid strode back into the room carrying a silver serving tray laden down with a coffee pot and several coffee mugs. Dora studied the senator and his wife as the maid poured five cups of coffee. The senator looked broken and more than a little devastated. The senator's eyes were red rimmed, and it was clear he'd been crying. His wife was also visibly upset, but Mrs. Quitoni's expression was determined, her eyes were clear, and her makeup was perfect. They were both wearing suits, but the senator looked like he had slept in his while Mrs. Quitoni looked ready to hit the campaign trail.

The maid finished serving and left the room quickly.

Dora ignored her cup of coffee. "We'd like to ask you a few questions about your daughter."

Senator Quitoni sank deeper into the sofa, but his wife's back straightened. "Our daughter didn't do anything to deserve this."

"Of course she didn't, but knowing as much about her as possible might help us to locate the person who took her life."

Mrs. Quitoni frowned.

"We'll tell you whatever you want to know," Senator Quitoni said in a scratchy voice.

"Of course," Mrs. Quitoni quickly answered. "I'm just not sure we know anything that will help you."

Logan smiled tightly. "You'd be surprised about what could be helpful."

"When was the last time either of you saw your daughter?"

"Two nights ago. She came over for dinner."

"And how did she seem then?" Dora asked.

"Fine," the senator responded. "She seemed fine. Happy. She had plans to meet up with some friends after dinner."

"Do you know who those friends were?"

The senator shrugged. "Michelle was a grown woman. We tried not to pry into her life."

"You could try asking Eisha Steele. That's Michelle's best friend. They went to school together."

Dora jotted the name down. "And Michelle had been working at the Leonard Art Gallery, correct?" Dora had her notebook out and was taking notes.

"Yes. Michelle was an art history major at Georgetown." Senator Quitoni rubbed his temples.

"She got her MBA at George Mason last year," Mrs. Quitoni rushed to add. "She had plans to own her own gallery. She didn't just want to look at pretty things her whole life—she had real plans for success."

"Veronica," the senator hissed at his wife.

It sounded as if Mrs. Quitoni wasn't totally on board with her daughter's career choices. It might be worth looking more closely into the family's dynamics. Discreetly, of course. She made a mental note of that thought rather than writing it down.

Dora plowed ahead with her questions. "Michelle had recently moved out on her own, I understand."

Senator Quitoni nodded. "Yes. She lived here through undergraduate and graduate school, but she was twenty-six. She wanted her own space. We bought her a town house downtown, not far from the gallery."

Which would have cost big bucks, probably well into the millions. She wasn't exactly making it on her own.

"You must have been close." She had to tread carefully, but Michelle's parents were two of the last people who'd seen her alive. Dora needed to get a better picture of the dynamics of their relationship. As sick as it sounded, most murder victims were killed by the people closest to them— husbands, wives, lovers, siblings, even children. It would not be the first time that a parent had killed a child.

Senator Quitoni focused on the wall of glass windows looking out onto a pool and beyond. "Our relationship was fine. Maybe a little complicated."

Mrs. Quitoni tensed at her husband's words. He might have been the elected representative, but it was clear she was the power behind the couple.

"Michelle is our only child, Detective," the Senator continued. "We were close when Michelle was young. Then I decided to run for office when she was a teenager. All the attention was difficult for her."

"She hated it," Mrs. Quitoni said, as if a teenage girl not liking media attention was some sort of sacrilege. Dora wasn't sure there were any teens who would appreciate going through puberty under a media microscope.

The room was silent for a moment.

"Is that why Michelle moved to London?"

"Yes," the senator answered.

"No," Mrs. Quitoni said at the same time.

Dora shared a look with Logan.

Mrs. Quitoni shot a glare at her husband, and he shrunk even farther into the sofa cushions. "Michelle got a fellowship at the Louvre. It was an opportunity of a lifetime."

"She went to London to get away from the media frenzy around my last campaign. It was bruising. My opponent accused me of accepting bribes in exchange for voting on certain bills. There was no evidence, of course, because it didn't happen, and the Senate ethics committee cleared me, but the media spent weeks speculating. It almost certainly would have cost me the election if it hadn't come out that my opponent was the one actually taking bribes."

"What is it they say?" Mrs. Quitoni smirked. "Every accusation is a confession."

Politics was hard to avoid in Washington, DC, especially when a sitting congressman was accusing the senator from his own state of taking bribes. The scandal had been in the news for weeks before the election, and the late-night comedians had a field day when it came out that the congressman was arrested for bribery. He'd resigned his seat and slunk out of Washington, leaving the field clear for the senator's reelection.

"And she moved back to Washington six months ago?"

"Yes, her supervisor at the Louvre recommended her for the job at the Leonard Gallery."

"Did Michelle mention having any problems with anyone at the gallery? Or anyone at all?"

"No," the senator breathed. "She loved that job. Only had good things to say about it."

"What about someone special in her life? A boyfriend or girlfriend?" Logan pressed.

"No." Mrs. Quitoni waved the suggestion away. "Michelle was focused on her career. She didn't have time for romance."

Dora and Logan shared another look. Young women didn't always share their love lives with their parents. They'd have a talk with Michelle's coworkers and best friend. They'd likely know if there was a special someone in Michelle's life.

Senator Quitoni dropped his head into his hands as if it was all too much. His wife patted his shoulder absentmindedly, the first show of affection Dora had seen between the couple since the interview had started.

"We understand you have identified a witness. Have they been able to tell you anything about the person who did this to our daughter?" Mrs. Quitoni turned her hard gaze on Dora.

Irritation stabbed through Dora's gut. They hadn't released information about a witness, for obvious reasons. That the Quitonis knew about the witness wasn't a shock, but it did mean that someone in the department was telling tales out of school. And because she had no doubt that someone had probably been in the morning meeting and sat several notches above her in the food chain, there wasn't likely to be a whole lot she could do about it.

"I'm not at liberty to discuss the details of the investigation."

"This is our daughter!" Mrs. Quitoni's voice shook.

"I understand that, ma'am. And I am going to do everything I can to bring her killer to justice."

"We understand that you want answers," Logan jumped in, "but revealing details could jeopardize the case."

The senator lifted his head and speared Dora with a look. "You can't believe we'd do anything that might let this animal get away with what they did to our—" Senator Quitoni's voice broke.

"Of course they don't." Mrs. Quitoni's patting picked up speed. Anger flashed in her eyes. "I think my husband needs to rest now. You two can see yourselves out."

She said it like a woman who was used to people doing what she told them.

Dora and Logan rose.

"Again, we are sorry for your loss," Logan said. "And we'll be doing everything we can to find out who took her from you."

"What do you think?" Logan said after they'd slid back into the sedan.

Dora started the car before turning in her seat to face him. "I think there's a lot the Quitonis aren't telling us."

Logan's smile was grim. "I think you're right."

Chapter Eight

The Sutton Place townhomes were modern builds with gray stones and faux-wood doors with solar panels on their roofs. They reminded Logan of *The Jetsons*. It was a secure community, but there had been no one at the guard's hut when they drove through the open gates. But when they pulled to a stop in front of Michelle's unit, a small electric vehicle stopped behind them and a man in khakis and a polo shirt with *Sutton Place* etched over his left breast got out.

"This is a private community. You need to leave," he said, storming toward the sedan as soon as Dora stepped out of the car. He was in his early thirties, with wavy dark brown hair and dark eyes to match. He wore a pronounced scowl.

She held out her badge. "I'm Detective Madison. This is Special Agent Elkins."

"Oh." The man visibly relaxed. "Sorry. I've been dealing with calls from the residents about the press sneaking in here all day." The man swiped at the sweat beading on his forehead. "The homeowners don't want me to close the gates. They'd have to use their key card, and that would be an inconvenience to them. Tell me how I'm supposed to keep people out, then, huh?"

"I'm sorry to hear that Mr.—" Dora said.

"Waylen Osvolo. I'm the property manager here." Osvolo's eyes narrowed. "So, you're the detective in charge of Michelle's case?"

"I am," Dora responded.

"And you're FBI?" Osvolo turned to Logan.

"I am."

"Well, how can I help? Michelle was a nice girl. I couldn't believe it when I heard—"

Dora rounded the car and headed for the front walk. Logan and Osvolo followed. "How did you hear about Michelle's murder?"

It hadn't escaped Logan's notice that Osvolo was referring to Michelle by her first name. It raised questions, like how well did the property manager know Michell Quitoni? He'd have to wait until Dora finished her line of questioning to get his answers, though.

"One of the vultures. They've been hanging around since early this morning, looking for anyone who will talk to them. One even tried to bribe me into letting them into Michelle's unit." Osvolo puffed out his chest. "Of course, I said no. Told that creep if I caught him around here again, I'd call the cops on him."

"As you should have," Dora responded.

Osvolo's chest puffed out more.

"Mr. Osvolo, these are town houses." Logan stopped at the bottom of the staircase leading to the front door of the unit. Dora started up the stairs but turned back when he spoke. "What sort of property management do you do for the residents?"

"Anything that needs doing." He chuckled. "The people that live here are rich—like, seriously rich. They don't want to worry about yard maintenance or busted pipes or missing roof shingles. The management company offers full-service property upkeep and maintenance. We take care of hiring contractors for your everyday maintenance, like mowing the lawn in the summer and shoveling the walkways in the winter, as well as plumbing, heating, and electrical emergencies. All the homeowner has to do is give me a call. We have a bevy of contractors on retainer."

"Sounds like my kind of homeownership," Dora quipped.

"And how much does service like that run the homeowners?" Logan asked.

"Well, the monthly homeowner's association fees run twenty-three hundred a month, not including special assessments."

Dora let out a low whistle. "Never mind."

Logan chuckled. "What kind of special assessments?"

"Well, if the pipe in your home burst, it wouldn't be fair for all the homeowners to pick up the cost."

"So, twenty-three hundred is your base cost per month. You'd likely have additional charges during a year because something is always going wrong in a house."

Osvolo nodded. "Exactly." The property manager leaned in and dropped his voice. "Some of the homeowners are constantly calling for one thing or the other. Little things. Like, just the other day, Mrs. Celetano called me to change her light bulb. Can you believe it? The management company charges a hundred fifty dollars every time I step foot into a unit, and she called me to change a light bulb. Rich people." Osvolo shook his head in disgust.

"Mr. Osvolo, you seem to know Michelle Quitoni pretty well," Logan said while the other man's head was still going back and forth.

Osvolo startled, just as Logan had hoped. He wanted

to catch the man off guard and gauge his reaction to the question.

Osvolo's neck pinked. "I... I don't know what you mean. She was a homeowner here. We were friendly, but nothing more than that."

Logan leaned against the stair railing. "You seem more than just friendly. For instance, you referred to Mrs. Celetano using an honorific and her last name, but you call Miss Quitoni by her given name, Michelle."

"I... It's... She told me to. It's not against the rules!" The pink from Osvolo's neck crawled upward.

"No one is suggesting you broke any rules, Mr. Osvolo." Dora stepped down a stair. "We're just trying to get a mental picture of Michelle's life. She has friends and acquaintances. The people she came into contact with regularly."

"Well, I only saw her on maintenance calls or if I happened to be driving by or manning the guard booth. That's all."

"Was she friendly with any neighbor in particular?"

He shook his head, still upset. "Not that I know of. I don't spy on the residents."

"We're not suggesting you do," Logan said in his most soothing voice. Osvolo certainly riled quickly.

"Did you ever see Miss Quitoni with anyone in particular? A boyfriend? A girlfriend?"

Another head shake. "No boyfriend. There is a girl sometimes, a woman, about the same age. They seemed like friends, though."

"Can you describe her?" Dora took out her notebook.

Osvolo's brow scrunched. "Blond hair, about down to here." He dusted his shoulder with his hand. "Close to Michelle's height. Pretty enough. Slim. Dressed really nice.

That's about all I remember. I only saw her a couple of times."

"This is great—thanks. And when was the last time you saw Miss Quitoni?" Dora asked, not looking up from her notebook.

Logan couldn't help but admire her technique. Slipping in the real question she wanted answered so smoothly.

Osvolo's body tensed. "I already told the officers that came by this morning. I was in bed asleep with my wife when Michelle was killed."

Dora lifted her head and pinned Osvolo in her gaze. "We don't know when Miss Quitoni was killed. Do you?"

"I... I meant..." Osvolo sputtered, and Dora let him. "Of course not. You're trying to confuse me. The reporters said you found her this morning. I meant to say I was in bed when you found her. And I'm sure I have an alibi for whenever she was killed—not that I need one. I didn't kill her!"

The slam of a car door had him spinning. Logan looked over Osvolo's shoulder. Three houses down, a woman wrangled a car seat out of the back of a Mercedes SUV. She didn't seem to be paying any attention to them.

Osvolo faced Logan and Dora again. "Look, I... I've told you everything I know."

Dora smiled. "But you haven't, Mr. Osvolo. You haven't answered my last question."

"Your question?" He wiped the sweat from his brow with his forearm. "What question?"

"When did you last see Miss Quitoni?"

"Um...maybe two, three days ago. In passing," he hurried to add. "It was trash day. Mr. Levin uses a walker and can't get around too well anymore, so I pull his trash cans to the curb for him. I headed to his house around seven that morning to make sure the trash got out before the men came for it, and I saw Michelle getting into her car. I waved, and she waved back. Her car was gone when I came back down the street about ten minutes later. I assumed she'd left for work."

Dora finished noting everything he'd said and closed her notebook. "Thank you very much, Mr. Osvolo. If I have any more questions for you, I know how to contact you."

It was a dismissal, and Osvolo seemed more than happy to heed it. He bounded down the walk. His car peeled away as Dora keyed in the code to get the key for the lock the uniforms had put on Michelle's door earlier that day.

Police protocol would have had uniforms out to Michelle's house soon after her body was identified to secure it.

Logan accepted the nitrile gloves Dora handed him as they passed through the doorway and snapped them over his hands.

The main floor was open space with the living area flowing into the dining area and into the kitchen. It wasn't a large space, but whoever had designed it had done the most with what they had. The space could have used some interior decorating. It looked more like a showroom than a home. A beige silk sofa sat atop a soft chenille rug with a glass coffee table anchoring the space. The obligatory flat-screen television was mounted on the wall across from the sofa. Under the large window, looking out onto the front lawn, sat a white desk, its top devoid of anything other than a small gold lamp.

"What are we looking for?" Logan asked.

Dora strode forward, speaking to him without turning around. "You know as well as I do it's always somewhat of a 'you'll know it when you see it' situation. Mostly, I just wanted to see Michelle's living space. Get a feel for how she lived." Dora glanced at him over her shoulder. "I figured you'd want to do the same, profiler."

Logan felt his brow arch.

"I may have read one or two of your papers." She turned around, but before he caught the hint of a smile on her face.

He couldn't help but feel good that she'd thought about him after they'd broken up, at least enough to keep up with his career after their breakup. He'd thought about her a lot. More than he cared to admit, even to himself.

"CSI has already been here and collected Michelle's tablet."

Logan opened the drawer of the desk seated under the window. Monogrammed letterhead and envelopes, paperclips, two pens with *Leonard Gallery* spelled out in cursive on their sides, and a highlighter were all that was inside the drawer.

The bookshelves on the opposite side of the room were orderly, organized by the author's last name. One shelf held a photo of Michelle and her parents and another of Michelle and a blonde woman, both women smiling widely and wearing bikinis on what looked like a very expensive yacht.

Logan picked up the photo. "This could be the blonde woman that Osvolo saw." He took his phone from his jacket pocket and snapped a photo before passing the photo to Dora, who did the same.

"Could be the best friend, Eisha Steele, that her parents told us about. I'll check into it when we get back to the station."

She replaced the photo on the shelf and headed for the stairs.

Logan followed.

There were three bedrooms upstairs, although one of the three was tiny. Michelle seemed to have agreed. She'd turned it into a closet.

Dora made a circle around the room. "If I counted all the clothes I've ever owned together, I don't think it would amount to this much."

Logan couldn't disagree. It was a lot of clothing. Dresses, skirts, and tops. Fancy, business, or casual. Michelle Quitoni could have opened a boutique just consisting of her wardrobe. It was overkill if you asked him. He had five suits—two black, two blue, and one tan.

They left the closet and headed for Michelle's bedroom. Like the rest of the house, it looked unused. The bed was made with military-sharp corners. End tables stood on either side, but their tops were clear of clutter.

Dora opened the closet door. Shelves of shoes stared back at her.

Logan went to the end tables. If there was anything to be found in a bedroom, the end tables, closets, and between the mattresses were where it would be found. The drawers in the end table were empty. Dora helped him shove the mattress to the side even though she protested that if there had been something to find, CSI would have found it. He didn't doubt CSI's professionalism, but he wanted to see it with his own eyes. There was nothing.

The attached bathroom and second bedroom were equally devoid of anything that could be useful.

"There is nothing here," Dora said once they'd descended the stairs.

"Yes and no," Logan responded.

Dora gave him a silent look.

"A home this clean, this unlived in tells me quite a bit about its inhabitant."

Dora fisted a hand on her hip and smirked. "Oh, really, and what had it been saying to you?"

Logan couldn't help grinning. "It tells me that Michelle was well ordered, likely a creature of habit. She liked that her life was orderly and neat. She's not likely to take many risks or veer off the path that she's set for herself."

"Okay." Dora drew out the word, letting him know that she wanted him to say more.

"I don't see her going off with someone she didn't know."

"So, she likely knew her killer, or at least was familiar with the person."

"I'm still gathering information, but this house—" he did a three sixty turn "—is the house of a woman used to being in control of her life. A woman that most likely sticks to a strict self-imposed schedule."

Dora clucked her tongue and headed for the front door. "Well, that's good at least. It means we just have to keep digging into Michelle's life. That's where we'll find our killer."

THE ITCH WAS BACK. That need. It was almost a command.

Find her.

He could feel it slowly rising up, humming through his body. Demanding action. He had to keep going until he found her. He had to keep going until he saved her. Then they could be together again.

A family, just like they used to be. He'd been mistaken about the others. He thought they were pure, like his own Sarah. But he was wrong.

He couldn't be wrong this time. He'd find her.

And then he would finally be free.

Chapter Nine

Landon felt bad about having Logan ask Dora for a favor. He knew his brother still had feelings for the pretty police detective. He hoped they could work out their differences. His brother deserved happiness, and Dora seemed to make him happy. It helped that the detective wouldn't stand for Logan's broody, silent act.

But it had been twenty years of not knowing exactly what had led to his father's death. Landon had always wondered. He'd always had his suspicions that his father's murder hadn't been a random robbery, and when he'd found his dad's hidden journal, his concerns had heightened even more. Well, he was an investigative reporter, after all. It was in his blood to sniff out a story.

So, he'd do what he had to do and make his apologies later, he thought as he headed to the basement of *The District Sun*'s offices.

The long windowless corridor leading to the *Sun*'s archive room was desolate so late in the evening. *The District Sun* was a small, though highly regarded, operation. What it lacked in operating funds, it made up for by hiring dogged, experienced professionals. But that meant savings had to be found wherever possible, and one area was with respect to archiving old articles and editions of the paper.

There was no money for cloud storage for everything, so the publisher kept files from the early 2000s on an in-house hard drive. It was rudimentary, but it worked. Articles from 2002, the year Addison Kober had gone missing, would be found on that hard drive.

The door to the archive room was kept locked, but Landon had gotten the key from the *Sun*'s receptionist before she left for the evening. The unfinished, dimly lit room was an open cavernous space that held rows of steel shelving with cardboard boxes stacked on them. Landon ignored the shelves and boxes. They held old, printed newspapers, notes of long-dead reporters, and who knew what else. What he needed might not have been accessible on the cloud, but it was accessible on the hard drive of the archive's old IBM computer.

The computer sat in the corner of the room on a beat-up wooden desk, beige monitor and matching beige keyboard.

Landon had to wait for what felt like a lifetime for the computer to boot up, but the screen finally lit up with the paper's logo and a box asking for his username and password. He entered his information, and after several more painstaking seconds, the search page appeared. He started with a broad search, entering the name *Addison Kober*. The search returned more than a dozen results. For the *Sun*, that was a lot of stories on the same topic. But the disappearance of Addison Kober had been big news in the Washington, DC, area two decades earlier.

He read through several of the articles, sending them all to his email before also sending them to the aged printer next to the desk.

He'd go through them all again more carefully, but for now, he wanted to gather as much information as possible. He noted the dates on the articles and the fact that as time wore on, fewer and fewer articles had been written about Addison. The last article written appeared approximately three months after Addison had gone missing. Three months. That was all the time it had taken for most of the world to forget about the disappearance of a fifteen-year-old girl.

He did another search, this one combining Addison's name with *William Burgess*. There were no hits. He tried similar searches with all the Burgesses and got the same result.

So, what had his father known that no one else did?

Landon logged off the computer and headed back upstairs to his desk. He wanted to do the same searches in the broader multi-newspaper databases that the *Sun* subscribed to, but he was sure those searches would return hundreds of results, if not more. He'd need to read through all of them. He'd learned early in his career to take nothing for granted. You never knew where the key to a story would be found. He'd pull every thread until he was sure where it led. Especially since he suspected one of the threads would lead him to his father's killer.

"I can't believe this is happening." Eisha Steele took another tissue from the box on the coffee table in front of the couch where she sat.

Dora had called ahead to let her know she and Logan would be stopping by, but Eisha had still burst into tears the moment she'd opened the door to them. She was clearly a woman overcome with grief, but she'd assured them that she would do whatever she could to help find Michelle's killer.

And Dora was hopeful Eisha knew something that

would help. She was the last person that they know of to have seen or spoken to Michelle before she was killed.

Dora sat beside Eisha on the sofa while Logan discretely roamed the living room.

"I'm sorry." Eisha sniffed. "It's just so unbelievable. Michelle is dead. No matter how many times I say it, it just doesn't feel real."

"Give it time. Let yourself grieve."

"Thank you."

"I'm sorry to have to do this now, but the sooner we can get some answers, the more likely we'll find the person that did this to Michelle."

Eisha nodded. "I totally understand. I want to help you."

"Thank you. Can you tell me how long you and Michelle have been friends?" She found it was somewhat easier to talk to family and friends of victims in the present tense, especially when the loss was hitting them hard. The past tense was a reminder that could sometimes overwhelm the person before she'd finished her questioning.

"We met in grad school. We were both getting our MBAs and had a couple of classes together. We hit it off and kept up the friendship after we graduated last year."

"Do you go out together a lot?"

"I wouldn't say a lot. We both have full-time jobs now. It's not like being in school. But we get together a couple times a month, usually for dinner but sometimes to hit a club, like the other night."

Dora made a note, then said, "Can you take me through what you two did, from the moment you met until you parted?"

Eisha took a deep breath and let it out slowly. "I'd gotten two VIP tickets to Vibe." She must have read the incomprehension on Dora's face because she followed up with,

"It's this new club in Northeast. Everyone's been talking about it, but it's pretty hard to get in, especially to the VIP section, where everyone wants to be seen. Anyway, this guy from work has been chatting me up, and I think he is working up to asking me out and wants to impress me. When he offered to get me two passes, to be honest, I didn't think he would do it, but I was super excited when he did."

"And Michelle went with you."

Eisha nodded. "She didn't really want to. I had to beg her to go, but she finally agreed."

"Why didn't she want to go?"

Frown lines formed on Eisha's forehead. "She'd been kind of weird lately. Like, not wanting to go out much. Preoccupied. At first, I thought it was just work, but she never wanted to talk about it when I asked, and that wasn't like her."

"Not to talk about her feelings?"

"Not talking about her feelings about work. She loved her job, even though she always butted heads with her boss about the best way to run the gallery." Eisha's gaze darted away before landing on Logan and Dora again. "John Leonard knows his art, but he's not a very good businessman. Michelle was always proposing new ways to get people into the gallery to get the gallery out in the community. But Leonard wanted to be exclusive. Very elite, but elite wasn't paying the bills."

"The gallery was in trouble?" Logan plucked a book from the bookshelf across from the sofa.

Eisha looked at him, a flash of surprise crossing her face as if she'd forgotten he was in the room. "*Trouble* may be overstating it. John comes from money, so I doubt he's in any danger of having to close, but the gallery isn't running in the black—that's for sure. Michelle was very vocal about what she would do differently when she had her own gallery. And now she'll never—" Eisha choked off a sob.

Dora gave her a minute to pull herself together before getting the interview back on track. "So, while you were at the club, any behavior in particular stand out at all to you?"

Eisha dabbed at her eyes. "I mean, Michelle was quieter than usual. She's usually up for dancing, but she rejected every guy that asked. She drank more than usual."

Dora jotted that information down. "How many drinks would you say?"

"Oh, I'm not sure. I didn't keep an eye on her all night. Now I wish I had." Eisha swallowed hard. "I know she had at least three over the night."

"And how long were you two there?"

"We got there about eleven. Dylan, the guy I mentioned, the one who gave me the tickets, was there. I ended up hanging out with him for a long time." She blushed. It seemed that the tickets had worked their magic. "I guess it was about one when Michelle said she was ready to leave. I was still having a good time and didn't want to go. Dylan offered to drive me home, so Michelle left."

"You two drove in her car to the club?" Logan said, giving Dora a pointed look.

"Yes. Michelle insisted." Eisha pulled a face. "I figured it was because she planned to leave early, which is why I wasn't that upset when she said she was going."

They hadn't found Michelle's car, and the killer would have had to get her to the park somehow.

"Do you remember anyone at the club paying special attention to Michelle? Asking her to dance a lot? Buying her drinks? Or just maybe hanging around?"

Eisha chuffed a laugh. "It's a club, Detective, and we were dressed for going out. Lots of guys paid Michelle special attention. I can't think of anyone that seemed creepy, though, and I'm sure she would have mentioned it if anyone had given her the willies."

"Okay, what about Michelle's love life more generally? Had she been seeing anyone lately?"

Eisha shook her head. "No. She'd gone on a few dates in the last year, but since grad school she hadn't seen anyone seriously. She, and I," she hurried to add, "have been mostly focused on our careers. There hasn't been time for romance."

"Is Michelle close to anyone else? Maybe someone from her job?"

"I think there's a part-time person that covers for Michelle when she takes a day off or when John goes out of town on a buying trip." Eisha didn't look at them while she answered.

Dora's cop instinct pinged. She shared a look with Logan and gathered that he'd also gone on alert. Eisha wasn't telling them something. She'd also looked away when she'd mentioned Michelle's contentious relationship with her boss.

Dora cleared her throat. "And her boss, John Leonard? You mentioned that Michelle butted heads with him. Was there more to their relationship?"

Eisha continued to avoid looking at either of them. "I'm not sure what you mean."

"I think you are," Logan responded.

Eisha heaved a sigh. "Look, John and Michelle spend a lot of time together at the gallery. I wasn't lying when I said they were at odds about how to run the place, but you know there's a thin line between love and hate and all that. She and John had gotten together a few times."

"Gotten together," Dora pressed. "You mean they were having an affair?"

Eisha rolled her eyes. "Affair may be too strong a word for it. They hooked up whenever the mood struck. It wasn't like they were in a relationship or anything though. I know Michelle saw other people. And John is technically married."

Dora wondered how someone could be technically married. In her book, you either were or were not married—it was pretty simple. But Eisha Steele's philosophy on commitment wasn't relevant to the case so she let it go. John Leonard was already on the growing list of people Dora needed to speak with.

"The only other person that Michelle talks about is her psychiatrist," Eisha added.

"Michelle was seeing a psychiatrist?" Logan sat the book down and moved over to the sofa. "Do you know why?"

Eisha shifted on the couch. "Not exactly."

Dora shot Logan a look she hoped he read correctly as *Back off* before focusing back on Eisha. "Eisha, I'm sure that you want to protect Michelle, but holding back information from us now doesn't protect her. But it may protect the person that killed her."

Eisha hesitated for a moment longer.

"I know Michelle struggled some with anxiety and depression while we were in graduate school. Her parents, her mother especially, put a lot of pressure on her to be perfect. The perfect student. The perfect businesswoman. To never do anything that anyone could perceive as embarrassing to the senator. Especially during his last campaign. The media was brutal, and Michelle didn't escape their glare."

"Did anything in particular happen during the senator's campaign that Michelle was concerned about?" Logan pressed.

Eisha shrugged. "I mean, the usual. Reporters followed her everywhere she went after the allegations against the senator came out. The campus police had to ban them, but that didn't help when she wasn't on campus."

"Do you know Michelle's psychiatrist's name?"

"Dr. Najimy."

Dora jotted down the name. "Did her parents know she was seeing a psychiatrist?"

"Definitely not," Eisha said emphatically. "Her parents wanted everyone to think they were this close, happy family, but Michelle could barely stand her mother, and she thought her father was weak and needed to stand up to her more."

Mrs. Quitoni definitely drove the relationship, based on what Dora had seen. Maybe the picture that the Quitonis had painted of their family wasn't as rosy as they'd have liked Dora to believe.

"So, Michelle left the club about two in the morning," Dora said, wanting to make sure that she didn't miss any of the details. "Did you speak with her or communicate with her at all after that?"

"I sent her a text just after four, letting her know I'd gotten home safely. We always did that for each other. I didn't hear back from her. Come to think of it, she never sent me a text telling me that she'd made it home safely. I should have noticed." Tears streamed down her face. "I could have called the police earlier, maybe…"

Dora reached for the woman's hand. "None of this is your fault, and I am sure that Michelle wouldn't want you blaming yourself."

Eisha's tears kept coming.

Dora suspected she wasn't going to get anything else out of her until she'd had more time to process her loss.

Chapter Ten

Logan wished he could say he was shocked by the news that Michelle might have been having an affair with her boss, but he wasn't. The picture of Michelle Quitoni that was emerging was that she was a woman with secrets. Dora got the contact information for John Leonard, owner of the Leonard Gallery and Michelle's boss, but he did not answer his cell or his office number. She left messages on both voicemails.

They had better luck when it came to Michelle's psychiatrist, Bruce Najimy. He agreed to fit them in between patients. They headed for his offices in Arlington, Virginia, after leaving Eisha.

Najimy's office was on the third floor of a medical building that housed a medical practice, psychotherapist's office, and a physiotherapist. The building was just on the other side of the Potomac from Washington, DC, in Virginia. Dr. Bruce Najimy was in a session when Logan and Dora arrived. Najimy's secretary, a rail-thin young man in his twenties with jet-black hair, offered coffee and tea and, after they'd declined, left them to wait in an elegantly furnished waiting area. The door to the interior office opened ten minutes later, and Dr. Bruce Najimy stepped out. A large window in the area overlooked the Potomac, a view that Logan was sure had added a few thousand dollars a year to the rent on the space.

"Detective Madison, please come in. Sorry for the wait." Dr. Bruce Najimy ushered them into the office. He waved them to the visitor's chairs in front of his desk. On the other side of the large office was a plush, upholstered sofa that faced a straight-backed armchair. End tables stood on either side of the armchairs with a brass lamp on one. This was obviously the space in the office where the doctor met with his patients.

"Thank you for seeing us on short notice, Dr. Najimy. This is Special Agent Logan Elkins. He's assisting the department with this case. He's a profiler with the FBI."

Logan shook the hand the doctor had offered.

"Happy to be of help, as you know, Detective," Dr. Najimy said.

"In addition to his private practice, Dr. Najimy assists the department from time to time when we need a psych evaluation."

"Forensic psychology has always fascinated me," he explained. "I enjoy the work, and it makes me feel as if I'm contributing to making the world a better place, so why not?"

"The department is lucky to have you," Dora said with a tense smile. "Hopefully, you can help us out with our investigation into Michelle Quitoni's murder."

"As much as I would like to help you, Detective Madison, Michelle was my patient. There's not a lot I can say given doctor-patient confidentiality."

"Your patient is dead, Doctor," Logan said, letting the irritation he felt creep into his tone. "I'd think that would take precedence."

"Special Agent Elkins, as a profiler, I'm sure you know

that confidentiality doesn't end with the patient's death. Unless Michelle or her representative gives me permission, I am limited in what I can say to you."

"Michelle is dead," Logan shot back bluntly. "I'm sure she would like her killer to be found and held responsible. Preferably before he or she kills again."

"Logan," Dora hissed, shooting him a quelling look before turning to the doctor. "Doctor Najimy, please, whatever you can tell us would be helpful."

"I'll do what I can."

"Could you tell us how long Michelle had been seeing you?"

"About six years." Najimy said.

"Six years?" Dora said, surprised.

So, while Michelle was an undergraduate, which most likely meant her parents knew about the therapy. After all, how would a college student have afforded the bill on her own?

Dora must have been thinking along the same lines. "Did Michelle's parents know she was seeing you?"

"I assume so. My bills are sent directly to Senator Quitoni's accountant and are always promptly paid."

"Do you know how she found you?" Logan asked.

Najimy leaned back in his chair and looked up at the ceiling in thought. After a moment, he said, "I believe it was through a referral, although I can't tell you who exactly."

Can't or *won't*. Either way Logan was sure it didn't matter. Najimy wasn't going to give them any more information than he wanted to, and he didn't appear to want to give them much. The psychiatrist was smug.

"How was Michelle's relationship with her parents?" Logan asked.

Najimy held up a finger and waved it from side to side. "Ah, ah, ah. That would be crossing the line."

"How about something easier?" Dora interjected before Logan could tell the psychiatrist where he could stick his finger. "When was the last time you saw Michelle?"

"I saw her twice a week, on Wednesdays and Fridays at noon."

"That doesn't answer the question," Logan shot back.

Najimy smiled. "You're correct, Special Agent Elkins. My apologies for not being precise. The last time I saw Michelle was Friday morning. It was our regularly scheduled appointment."

"Did she seem worried or upset?" Dora pressed. "Anything at all out of the ordinary with her?"

"Again, I can't get into the details of our session."

Logan started to speak.

Najimy forged ahead. "But Michelle seemed the same as she always did."

"Dr. Najimy, Michelle's best friend told us that she was seeing you for anxiety and depression."

Najimy blinked but did not speak.

Logan sighed. "Look, can you at least tell us if you'd prescribed any medications for her? We'll find out whether she was on anything when the toxicology report comes back, but it would help to know what medications were supposed to be there to weed out those that shouldn't."

Najimy hesitated for a moment. "I have prescribed fluoxetine and diazepam."

Logan knew enough about pharmaceuticals to recognize the medications: Prozac and Valium.

"Do you know if she was having trouble with anyone? A boyfriend or lover? Maybe someone who wanted to be in those categories?"

"Not that I know of, but…" Najimy broke off. He stroked his beard with one hand.

"Doctor," Logan pressed.

"This is probably crossing a line, but Michelle had mentioned feeling as if someone was watching her."

Dora leaned forward in her chair. "Did she say who?"

"No, and to be honest, I didn't think much of it. Her father's election scandal was not easy for Michelle. The press was relentless. They followed her for weeks. For someone already suffering from anxiety and depression, it was trying."

Logan fought back a smile. Najimy didn't seem to realize he'd confirmed that Michelle was seeing him for anxiety and depression, though the medications he had her on were evidence enough.

"So, you don't think Michelle was actually being followed?"

Najimy held his hands up. "I don't know now."

A familiar hum vibrated in Logan's chest. This could be important. "And she gave you no indication of who she suspected of following her?"

"None whatsoever." The phone on the doctor's desk buzzed. "I'm sorry, Detective, Special Agent. My next patient is here." He rose and extended his hand over the desk. "If there is anything else I can do for you, please don't hesitate to let me know."

They shook hands, and Najimy led them to a different door than the one they'd come into the office through. It led directly into the building's hallway.

"What do you think?" Dora asked as they headed for the elevators.

"I think I don't like the good doctor."

She chuckled. "I'm with you there, but I meant what do

you think of what the doctor told us. About someone possibly watching Michelle."

"I don't know what to think. Najimy all but said Michelle was seeing him for anxiety and depression. It's possible she was paranoid."

"Possible, but you don't think so." The elevator doors opened, and they stepped out into the building's main lobby.

Logan watched Dora fall into step beside him. "I think it's all we have to go on right now."

MERCY'S BAR AND GRILL was located on Wisconsin Avenue in the upscale Friendship Heights neighborhood. The restaurant was already pretty busy by the time Dora arrived to meet with her best friend, Special Victims Unit Detective Noreen Montgomery. Noreen had already arrived and gotten a table for them.

Dora greeted her friend and took a seat, ordering a prosecco when the waitress stopped by the table. Noreen already had a glass of red wine in front of her.

While they waited for the waitress to return with Dora's drink, Noreen asked, "So, how are you doing?"

"The case? It's taxing. I can't stop thinking about the next victim."

"You never do. I've never met a more compassionate cop than you, even though you tried to hide it. But I was talking about how you are doing with Logan being back."

Dora rolled her eyes. "Of course you already know. Do you have spies everywhere?"

"Yes." Noreen laughed.

The waitress returned with Dora's drink and took their orders. They both got the surf and turf. When the waitress left, Noreen turned the conversation back to Logan.

"Okay, now spill. Is he still hot?"

"That is irrelevant," Dora replied, heat rising in her cheeks.

"You're blushing," Noreen teased, "so I'm going to take your nonanswer as a yes."

"Logan and I are over."

"Okay," Noreen said, incredulously taking a sip of her wine.

"It's been two years, Nor. I'm over him."

"It's been two years, but you are definitely not over him. You haven't seriously dated anyone since Logan moved to Arizona."

"That has nothing to do with him. I've been focused on my job."

"Yeah, right." Noreen snorted. "Keep telling yourself that. Maybe you'll believe it soon."

"It's true."

"Okay, listen, maybe it wouldn't be all that bad for you to explore a bit when it comes to Logan."

"Explore."

"Yes, I mean he's moved back to DC, right?"

"Yes."

"Well, if you wanted something to happen with him, the long-distance thing isn't an issue."

"He dumped me."

"I get it, and he's a fool for that. But did you tell me he said he was ending the relationship because he didn't think he could do long distance? That's not an issue now is all I'm saying."

"Maybe," Dora said, mostly because she didn't know if she wanted to go down that road. It might've been two years, but it wasn't all that easy to put herself out there again.

Noreen held her hands out in a surrender pose. "Okay, I'll back off. Just don't let the past be a barrier to your future."

Noreen didn't wait a beat before she launched into a story about her most recent date. Purposely changing the subject, Dora knew. For all her encouragement to get back together with Logan, Noreen enjoyed dating more than she enjoyed being in long-term relationships.

Dora listened and responded appropriately, but her mind still replayed what Noreen had said.

Was she letting her past with Logan keep her from envisioning what a future could be for them? More importantly, did she even want a future with him?

Chapter Eleven

When he'd informed his older brother, Landon, that he was moving back to Washington, DC, Landon had offered Logan the use of one of the spare rooms in his house. It was a nice offer and probably the only way he'd get to spend a good deal of time with his busy journalist brother, but Logan hadn't been able to see himself moving back into his childhood home. Especially not now when both his parents were gone. Just visiting Landon there brought back memories that could sometimes be overwhelming. He couldn't imagine living there again.

Instead, he'd rented an apartment in Southwest. The rent was a little pricy, but the neighborhood was convenient, and his building was only a two-block walk to the metro station. It meant he rarely had to drive the car he paid a small fortune to park in the building's garage. His sister, Lisa, had been after him to buy a house and really put down roots. He knew it made sense—more sense at least than paying rent forever. But he wouldn't consider buying a house until he was married and ready to start a family. And he'd only ever envisioned it happening in fleeting moments in what seemed to be a lifetime ago with Dora.

He strode through the building lobby and took the elevator to the seventh floor, heading for his corner apartment.

He could hear movement inside as soon as he opened the door. Someone was in his kitchen. He sniffed. Cooking.

Logan shut the door to his apartment and stepped into the galley kitchen. His niece, Layla, stood barefoot in front of the stove.

"Hi, Uncle Logan." Layla flashed a brilliant smile that turned his heart to putty. No matter how old she got, he'd always see the little girl that he'd bounced on his knee and given piggyback rides when she was little.

"I got hungry. I'm making pancakes." Layla expertly flicked her wrist, sending the pancake in the pan on the stove into the air and catching it like a pro. His niece loved to cook, much like her mother, and had recently begun thinking about going to culinary school when she graduated from high school in two years' time.

Logan dropped a kiss onto Layla's forehead. "Hmm. Smells good. Do you have enough for your old uncle?"

"Sure."

"Sweetheart, you know you're always welcome, but refresh my memory—did we have a playdate scheduled?"

Layla looked so much like her mother, his sister, Lisa. But she reminded Logan more of his older brother, Landon. Self-assured. Dogged when they thought they were right. Stubborn, even. It was that self-assuredness and doggedness that had made Landon a great investigative reporter. And it was Landon's stubborn streak that had kept him from giving up on investigating the nearly twenty-year-old murder of their father.

Layla rolled her eyes at him in perfect teenage fashion. "I am too old for playdates. Mom is making dinner for Edgar, and I didn't want to be there for that."

Logan's sister, Lisa, hadn't dated for years after her divorce, but she recently began venturing back onto the dating market. Edgar was a coworker that Lisa had begun seeing quite a bit of, much to her daughter's dismay.

"Ah, so you decided to pay me a visit. I'm sorry I wasn't here."

"It's no problem. I just borrowed the spare set of keys Mom has. Actually, I was supposed to go to Julia's house, but…" Layla shrugged.

Logan had spent enough time with the teen to know when a shrug was more than just a shrug. Julia was Layla's best friend, he'd gleaned from the number of times her name had appeared in Layla's stories.

"But what?" he pressed.

Layla shrugged again. "Julia is being kind of weird is all."

"Kinda weird how?"

"I don't know, just kind of…mean lately."

"She's being mean to you?" Logan's protective instincts piqued, though he reminded himself that Julia was a sixteen-year-old girl.

"Don't go all FBI man on me, okay?" Layla plated two pancakes and slid them across the bar to Logan. She grabbed her own plate and slid onto the bar stool next to him.

"I don't know what's going on with Julia." Layla spoke around the piece of pancake she just popped into her mouth. "She started hanging out with these other two girls, Marleen and Elyse."

Layla stuck her forefinger into her mouth and made a gagging noise.

Logan chuckled but kept eating. He'd learned it was best to let Layla talk things out herself. She was a bright girl who usually made it to the right decisions on her own.

"I don't know what Julia sees in them. They barely come

to school. I think they both had to do summer school, like, every year since the ninth grade. And they smoke, which is just gross." Layla made a face.

Logan's brow rose. "Smoke what?"

"Cigarettes is all I've seen them smoke, but I wouldn't be surprised if they smoked weed too. And..." Layla held up a hand. "Before you get upset, no, I have never and will never smoke cigarettes. They are truly nasty."

He thought about pressing the obvious omission of weed from her statement but then thought better of it, remembering Lisa saying she had to pick her battles.

"I don't know," Layla said forlornly. "I'm not sure Julia and I are friends anymore."

"I'm sorry, sweetheart. I think it would be Julia's loss, but I know saying that doesn't make it any easier when it feels like a friend is pulling away."

Layla wiped her eyes with the heel of her hand. Logan put down his fork and wrapped an arm around his knees. Despite all the talking she'd done, she also managed to clear her plate.

"Hey, I think I got some Ben and Jerry's Cherry Garcia in the back of the freezer."

The ends of Layla's mouth turned out just as he knew they would. Cherry Garcia was her favorite flavor of ice cream, which was why he always kept some on hand.

"What do you say you grab it and pick a movie to watch together?"

Layla pressed a quick kiss to his cheek before hopping from her stool and heading to the kitchen.

While she rooted through the freezer, he shot a quick text to Lisa, letting her know Layla was at his place and that he would drop her off at home after the movie. He'd missed a lot of time with his family while he'd been in Arizona, and he was happy to be making up for that now. He was getting closer to his sister and Layla, even if he still only saw Landon sporadically.

Dora's face flitted through his mind's eye. Hopefully, his family members weren't the only people he could rebuild bonds with.

"JUST RELAX. YOU'RE SAFE. No one can harm you here," Forensic artists Jacob Colson said in a calming voice.

Randi let out a shuddering breath.

"I want you to close your eyes and think back to Friday night," Jacob said. Dora knew there was much more to getting a good sketch from a witness than simply drawing. Jacob was one of the best sketch artists and interviewers on the force. If anyone could get Randi to give them something they could work with, it was Jacob.

Randi closed her eyes.

"Keep breathing. You're safe."

Randi took a deep breath and let it out.

"Tell me what you see."

"Nothing. It's dark."

"Okay. Where are you exactly?"

"At a picnic table." Randi's shoulders tensed and her face reddened. "I was smoking a joint."

"You're doing great, Randi." Dora spoke softly and encouragingly. Nobody in the department was going to care about their witness smoking weed. Not when a senator's daughter had been murdered.

"What do you hear?" Jacob continued the interview.

Randi frowned. "Cars, but they aren't close."

"Good. What else?"

"Something rustled in the bushes nearby. A squirrel or something."

"Good. Anything else?"

Randi sat up straighter. "A car door slammed."

That was new information.

"Okay. You're doing an amazing job," Jacob encouraged. "Now, when did you first notice the man?"

"I'm not sure. He was just there all of a sudden. Carrying something. I didn't know what."

"When did you realize he was carrying someone?"

"I didn't. I just… I don't know how to explain it. I just knew that he couldn't see me, so I ducked down under the table."

"All right. What happened next?"

"I watched from under the table. I remember thinking that he was going to hear me breathing. It sounded so loud to my ears."

"That's very common when we're in high-stress situations," Jacob assured her.

"I just stayed huddled under the table. He put her down on the grass and, like, smoothed her clothes. It looked like he might have put something in her hair, but I can't be sure. He…" Randi paused, a shiver rolling through her body. "He kissed her. Then he walked away. I… I stayed under the table for a while. I wasn't sure if he was going to come back or…or what."

"That's totally understandable. Smart. You did the right thing, protecting yourself."

"I didn't hear the car drive away or anything, but after a while I figured it was okay to come out. I wanted to run away, but I thought the woman might need help, so I went over to where she was. But she didn't look…"

Randi didn't have to finish the sentence. The first time seeing a dead body was traumatic. Heck, it was still traumatic for her, and she'd seen plenty of dead bodies. It never got easier realizing what humans were capable of doing to each other.

"I ran. I ran to the convenience store and called the police."

"Exactly what you should have done," Jacob said. "Can you tell me whether the man you saw was white, Black, or Hispanic?"

"It was a white guy."

"Okay." Jacob picked up his pencil. "And how about his size? Was he a large man? Thin? Tall? Short?"

Jacob led Randi through a series of questions, at times flipping through the extensive facial-identification book that she used to get facial features correct. The sketch took a little more than two hours, sketching and revising. The man had been wearing a knit cap, so they didn't have his hair style or color, and it had been too dark to see his eye color, but Jacob was knowledgeable in biometrics. Given the shape of the suspect's face, other features that Randi was able to pull from her memory and the fact that the overwhelming majority of people had brown eyes, Jacob sketched the man with darker irises. They'd leave eye color off the official description, though.

"What happens now?" Randi asked as Dora led her to the desk of the uniformed officer tasked with driving her back to Violet's house.

"Now you go home and get some rest."

Randi frowned. "I meant with the case."

Dora bit back a sigh. "I'm going to keep investigating."

Randi chewed on her fingernail. "Do you think my sketch is going to help you catch the guy?"

The truth was the sketch was pretty generic. A white man, average height, not thin, strong enough to carry dead weight about seventy-five yards from the park's parking lot to the field, possibly with dark features. It described a good portion of the male population.

"You've been a big help, Randi."

Randi crossed her arms over her chest. "I just want my life back. I know it might not seem like much, but I don't want to cower in some stranger's home with her hovering over me. I could have stayed at home with my mother if I'd wanted that."

That was probably exactly where she should have been. As was standard operating procedure, Keene had run a criminal background check on Randi. She'd grown up in a West Virginia suburb and had run away right before graduating from high school. Keene had tried reaching her mother, but the phone number they had was out of service. The local cops had gone to the last address on file, but the home was empty and didn't look to have been lived in for some time. So, Randi had become Dora's problem. Her criminal record indicated that she'd been arrested once for loitering and once for possession. Both charges were filed when she'd been a juvenile, and both charges had been dropped.

"Listen, we are going to everything in our power to find this guy. The best thing you can do is to go back to Violet's house. Stay there for the time being, so I know how to get in touch with you if I need you." An idea popped into Dora's head. "You know what? Wait here for a moment."

Dora hurried to her sergeant's desk. The department kept a few disposable cell phones on hand for use by confidential informants. Sergeant Harris wasn't at his desk, but everyone knew he kept the phones in the lower drawer of his desk. She plucked one from the desk, leaving a note for the sergeant to let him know she'd taken one of the phones, then headed back to Randi.

"Take this phone. You can use it to call me if you remember anything or if you need someone to talk to." Dora handed her the phone and another one of her business cards.

Randi turned the box over in her hands. "How do I even use it?"

"The instructions are in the box. It's easy. Come on." Dora put a hand on Randi's shoulder and led her to the uniformed officer.

Randi followed the officer out of the station, still looking skeptically at the cell phone box. At least it would give her something to do for a while.

Dora headed back to her desk. Logan sat at his desk, waiting.

"Jacob left copies of the sketch." Logan passed the sketch over to her.

She was struck again by the genericness of the likeness.

"Not much to work with," Logan said.

Dora massaged her temple. "No, no, it isn't. You want to come with me to tell Crenshaw the good news?"

"Uh…"

She dropped her hands to her side and gave him a pointed look. "Get up, Special Agent."

Logan grinned and stood.

Together, they marched across the bullpen floor. Crenshaw waved them in through the glass door.

"What do you have for me?"

Dora handed over the sketch.

Crenshaw studied the picture for a moment before tossing it onto her desk. "What the hell is this?"

Dora stood at attention in front of the lieutenant's desk. "The witness did the best she could, Lieutenant."

Crenshaw stabbed a finger at the sketch. "If this was

her best, I'd hate to see her worst. This could be any white man in Washington, DC." Crenshaw threw up her hands. "It could be *every* white man in Washington, DC."

Logan sat in a visitor's chair and crossed one leg over the other. "Lieutenant, your witness is a homeless seventeen-year-old young woman. It was dark, and she was scared. I'm surprised she was able to give us as much as she has. It is possible that, given some time, she'll remember more."

Crenshaw glared at Logan. "Special Agent Elkins, I—we—haven't been afforded that kind of time. The chief, the mayor, hell, I've even gotten calls from DC's congressional delegation. They are all on me to solve this thing. Now, today."

"In my opinion, we shouldn't release the sketch," Dora said. "You're right. It's too generic. All it's going to do is have every nosy Rosy calling in about their middle-aged male neighbor. We'll give her a few days. Maybe Logan is right, and Randi will be able to give us more detail."

Crenshaw shook her head and reached for the bottle of Tylenol on her desk. She swallowed two of them without water before speaking again. "I can't hold back the sketch." She held up a hand to hold off Logan's protest. "You should remember how things work around here. There's no way that half the bullpen doesn't already know about the sketch, which means that I can expect a call from the chief any moment now demanding a copy."

Logan groaned. "And there's no way he won't want to go out with it. Show the public that his department is making progress on the high-profile case."

Crenshaw pointed at him. "Exactly."

"We could try explaining to the chief. He understands

how investigations go. The need to keep some information close to the vest."

Crenshaw scowled. "I know you aren't that naive, Madison, so I'm going to chalk that comment up to exhaustion. Too bad you don't have time to rest up." The lieutenant planted her palms on the desk and pushed herself to her feet. "Look, the sketch is going out, probably by this afternoon, and it's going to be a crap fest. Prepare yourselves and keep doing your job. Dismissed." She sat back down heavily.

"Well, that went well," Logan said as they headed back to their desks.

Dora slid him a look. "It actually went better than I expected. Let's call the team together and do our jobs, Elkins."

Chapter Twelve

Dora headed back to her desk.

Logan followed her, thinking about his conversation with Landon. Now was as good a time as any to ask for a favor, he supposed. "I have a favor to ask," Logan said.

Dora didn't respond other than to raise her brows.

"You know about my father's murder, I assume."

He was sure she did. She was a cop, after all, and it would only take a Google search to find out about his father's murder. Logan hadn't spoken about it much at all while they'd been together. But she had mentioned once that he'd mumbled in his sleep, grief-stricken nightmares of a thirteen-year-old boy who lost his father.

Dora nodded.

"Landon wants to take a look at the police file. He's convinced he might see something no one else has that could maybe jump-start the case."

Dora was shaking her head before he finished the statement. "You know I can't do that. It is against a dozen rules and I'm not sure why he thinks he can find something no one else could. And find it twenty years later."

"I know it's a longshot and so does he. It's a huge ask. You don't owe me or my brother anything, but please, would you just think about it? I think if Landon could see the file, see that there is nothing there that could help him, maybe he could move on."

Lieutenant Crenshaw's voice boomed before Dora could speak again. "Madison. Elkins. Are you two going to join us, or what?"

Dora stood and hurried toward the conference room for the task-force meeting that was starting now.

Logan sighed, the weight on his shoulders growing, and followed her. Inside the conference room, he surveyed the attendees. Dora, Keene, Roberts, and Lieutenant Crenshaw were all present to get an update on where the case stood and get their marching orders. He was impressed with how Dora had handled the case so far, even if it hadn't completely been smooth sailing between them.

Dora started them off with an update on the toxicology report that had come in earlier that morning. The medical examiner had found antidepressants and antianxiety medications just like Najimy had warned. But the medical examiner had also found a mild sedative in Michelle's system that couldn't be explained. Michelle's car was also still missing, but they had received her phone records from her cell phone carrier. Eisha had told the truth about texting Michelle and not receiving a reply. Between late Friday night when Michelle and Eisha were at the club and when they had found Michelle's body, there were no outgoing calls or texts from the phone.

As they had feared, the brass had released the sketch of the suspect and the station's phones had been ringing off the hook since. Crenshaw had added several uniforms to the team, who had been tasked with weeding through the information that came in on the tip line and passing on anything that warranted further investigation.

After going over all the new and not terribly helpful information, Dora handed the meeting over to Logan.

"Let me start by saying that this is all preliminary. As we know more, I'll be refining and hopefully giving you a more helpful profile. Our witness reports seeing a white male. That's in keeping with the profile of the majority of serial killers. Our guy is probably between thirty and forty-five years old. He's going to be strong, strong enough to carry deadweight some distance, but unlikely to stand out in a crowd. All the victims are similar in age, size, and coloring—that is Caucasian females with brown hair. There's no known connection between the females, but when we catch the guy, we are likely to find some tenuous connection."

"Tenuous as in what?" Dora was taking notes.

"Something like all the women went to the same gym chain, even if not the same location. Or they all frequented the same coffee shop downtown. Something that is very difficult for the police to hit on but becomes obvious once you're told about it."

"But why these women specifically?" Detective Roberts asked.

Logan shifted his gaze to Roberts. "It's hard to say exactly, but since there is no obvious connection, most likely the women represent someone in the killer's life. Someone they love or loved, I'd think."

"Someone they loved," Keene said disbelievingly.

"There's a reason for the saying 'there's a thin line between love and hate,'" Logan responded. "Both can be very strong emotions."

He couldn't help a glance at Dora, but she did not look up from her notes. He continued.

"But in this case, the writing on the victims—'Protect

the innocent'—would suggest the killer sees these women as somehow wholesome or pure."

Roberts frowned. "But how would killing the women be protecting them?"

Logan was used to dealing with skeptics. Not everyone believed that profiling was real police work. He kept his voice measured. "Only the killer could answer that question for sure, but it could be any number of things. He could believe he's saving the women from having their innocence corrupted by killing them. Or he could believe them innocent when he kidnaps them, but then, for some reason, they displease him, and they are no longer pure in his eyes. I'm leaning in the direction of the latter explanation more than the former."

"Or," Roberts interrupted, "he could choose these women because he thinks that he is protecting some other person by killing them."

"That's possible," Logan conceded, even though his professional ire was up. "But I don't think it's likely in this case. Think about how he stages the bodies. He takes great care to dress them, pose them, and leave a flower in their hair, and even after he's brutalized them. That suggests feelings of rage and kindness in turn."

"It suggests to me that he's a sick monster," Roberts spat.

"That too. But he's also smart, probably employed, a seemingly normal guy," Logan said, getting back to his preliminary profile. "He has been smart enough to avoid leaving any evidence that could identify him. He plans these kidnappings and killings. So far, we have no witness to the actual abduction. He has to have somewhere safe and secure to take the women back to since he keeps them for two to three days. Probably a house, maybe in nearby Virginia or Maryland, since he would want some space to be sure the neighbors didn't see or hear anything suspicious."

Keene leaned forward in his chair. "We've got a witness now."

"Yes, and that might scare our guy. He's been getting bolder. He probably didn't expect anyone in the park the night he left Michelle. If your sketch is accurate—"

"A big if," Roberts interjected.

"If it's accurate, the unsub may panic. That could lead him to act out or to go into hiding."

"Not terribly helpful," Dora said.

"Sorry." Logan shrugged. "Again, not an exact science."

The meeting broke up soon after that. Dora sent Keene and Roberts out to re-canvass Michelle's neighborhood with the sketch in hopes that it would rekindle someone's memory. Michelle's boss, John Leonard, had finally responded to Dora's message, saying that he could meet with her at noon that day. She and Logan were bound for that meeting.

"You really know your stuff, Elkins," Dora said after everyone else had left the room.

"Did you almost choke on those words?" Logan teased.

A thin but genuine smile graced Dora's face.

Warmth bloomed in Logan's chest.

"Not as much as I thought I would have," she shot back. "I'm serious. You're very good at this."

"Thank you. You've done a fantastic job on this case."

The smile fell from Dora's face, and she sighed. "I feel like I am no closer to finding our killer than I was when we found our first victim. And that I'm running out of time before he takes his next victim."

"That's not on you. The killer is responsible for his actions."

"Yeah, well, tell that to the media, the public, and the Quitonis. If we don't find this guy soon, they are going to have all of our heads."

"Well, we'd better get to work, then."

"Kaj, just the man I'm looking for."

Kaj Ryland looked up from his computer and grinned. "Oh boy, now I know I'm in trouble."

The FBI's best tech analyst stood. It was like watching one of those tube men you saw in front of car dealerships unfold upward. Before joining the FBI, Kaj had played basketball in the Euro League. At seven feet two inches, a sitting Kaj was almost as tall as Logan, but a standing Kaj towered over both him and Dora. Basketball aside, Kaj had one of the finest minds for technology that Logan had ever encountered. He'd done wonders with video-enhancing technologies, including creating groundbreaking software. Rumor had it that Kaj was filthy rich and didn't have to work at all, much less for a federal salary. But he did it because he wanted to serve his country, which Logan could respect.

Kaj grabbed Logan's hand, pulling a man for a quick handshake and pat on the back before stepping back and taking in Dora.

Logan noted the pang of jealousy that shot through him and realized he didn't have a right to it. Still, he'd heard more than one of his female coworkers mention how attractive Kaj's wavy blond locks and blue eyes were.

"And who is this lovely lady?"

"Detective Dora Madison with the DC Metropolitan Police Department," Dora answered before Logan could.

"Well, Detective Madison, what can I do for you?"

"You can call me Dora."

Kaj's smile widened. "Dora, how may I be of service?"

"We need a video image cleared up, hopefully enough to make out the face of the person in it," Logan answered.

Kaj rolled his eyes. "Oh, is that all? You guys think this stuff is so easy. You just pop in here with a grainy video from some convenience store robbery and poof. I'm just supposed to pull whatever you need from it," Kaj said, just enough just to let Logan know that he wasn't really too put out.

"I don't think it's easy at all," Logan responded. "That's why I bring it to you, a master at what you do."

"Yes, yes, I'm Mr. Master Wizard. If you think flattery will get your job done faster, think again. Two tickets to next week's Washington Commanders game. On the fifty-yard line."

Logan crossed his arms over his chest and gave his friend a look. "That's blackmail and not only unbecoming of a federal employee, it's illegal."

"Well, I wouldn't want to break any laws. To the back of the line with you. Let's see... I should get to your case, oh, six months from Tuesday." Kaj grinned.

Logan tried and failed to beat back his own smile. "You're something else, you know that? I'll see what I can do, but they definitely won't be on the fifty-yard line. I'm collecting a civil-servant salary just like you."

"That sounds suspiciously like I shouldn't hold my breath," Kaj sighed dramatically. "What do you have for me?"

"It's a video of a female we believe is our victim being followed by an unidentified male," Dora answered.

Kaj's eyes lit with understanding. "Is this the serial killer case?"

"It is."

"Damn." Kaj looked from Dora to Logan. "You should have led with that. Forget the tickets. I want to get this guy off the street as much as anyone else. I have three sisters. How do you know the victim is in the video?"

"Well, as I said, it's grainy," Logan started.

"But," Dora interjected, "we know the store was the last place our victim was seen and based on the size, shape, and clothing of the female image in the video, we're pretty sure it's her."

"Okay." Kaj took the USB drive Logan handed to him. "I'll try to clean up the entire frame so you can be sure of both your victim and your unsub. I make no promises, and it may take a while. I have to get in there to see what I'm working with. Though store cameras are notoriously bad."

"I'd be grateful for whatever you could do." Dora smiled back at Kaj, and another jolt of jealousy hit Logan. He beat it back a second time.

"We have a forensic artist's rendering of a suspect from our witness," Logan said, forcing himself to focus on the case. He pulled out his phone and shot the sketch to Kaj's email.

The computer on the desk let out a jingling chime a moment later. Kaj reached for the mouse, opened the email, and popped the sketch up on the large monitor in front of them. He frowned. "You think this is your guy in the video?"

"Could be," Logan hedged.

"Kind of generic, but I'll keep it in mind."

"Thanks, Kaj."

"No problem." Kaj waved as they exited the office.

"This is the best evidence we have. Do you really think

your guy can clean up the video enough for us to get a look at our suspect?"

"If anyone can do it, it's Kaj."

Chapter Thirteen

Another one had failed. He watched the light drain from her eyes with sadness in his heart. Would he ever find someone worthy?

It wasn't enough that they look like his Sarah. His Sarah had been pure. Good. These women, they weren't good. They fought him. Even when he tried to explain he wouldn't hurt them. Not unless they didn't cooperate. Not while they behaved. But they never behaved.

Sometimes they pretended for a while. But they all tried to escape eventually. And that was when he knew. They would never measure up to Sarah.

That was when they had to go.

Michelle had been especially defiant. If he had known who she was, he would have never grabbed her.

He'd been more careful with this one. Christine. But it hadn't mattered in the end. He'd been forced to kill her too.

He took one last look at the dead woman. Her eyes were open, staring back at him.

The sound of footsteps startled him. He'd gotten a late start moving Christine's body to the park. It was starting to get light, which meant people.

The footsteps got louder. Closer. There wasn't time to lay this one out like the others.

He swore silently. He couldn't get caught. He needed to find his Sarah. He glanced one more time at the body in the trunk of the car, dismayed Christine wouldn't get the send-off she deserved.

Then he ran.

Hours of additional research had led Landon to Carisse Lynn's small sandwich-and-coffee shop in the Petworth neighborhood. The neighborhood was mostly residential, with many of the iconic row houses that frequently make their way into photos of Washington, DC. One of the main commercial areas ran along Georgia Avenue, which was where Carisse's sandwich shop, the Upper Crust, was located.

She'd been listed as the owner and manager on the website he found. Carisse had been a maid for the Burgesses around the time that his father appeared to have been investigating William Burgess. Questioning Carisse was a long shot, but it wouldn't be the first time that a long shot had paid off for him. And most people, especially rich people like the Burgesses, underestimated just how much of their business the hired help was privy to. Hopefully, Carisse could at least point him in the right direction. Any direction at all would be helpful at this point in his investigation. He felt like the investigation into his father's death was running on fumes.

The coffee shop was bright with tables covered with red-and-white checked tablecloth and a comfortable homey vibe. Midday on a weekday, it was fairly full, with most of the tables occupied and two people waiting in line when Landon entered.

He waited his turn and when he got to the head of the

line, he ordered the most expensive sandwich on the menu, artisan roast beef, and a root beer before asking for Carisse.

He took a seat at one of the last open tables and waited. After about ten minutes, a brunette woman in jeans, a white blouse, and sensible black sneakers headed toward his table with a loaded plate and a can of A&W root beer.

"Roast beef and a root beer. Don't get many requests for that anymore. Or many requests to see the manager before the customer has even gotten their food." Carisse eyed him warily. "How can I help you?"

"I'm sure the food is excellent. But I was hoping to speak to you about the time you worked for William Burgess," Landon said.

Carisse drew back in surprise. "Now, there's a name I haven't heard in decades. You know he's an ambassador to Ecuador or Iceland or somewhere."

"Australia," Landon corrected. "I'm an investigative reporter so I also know that you were a housekeeper for the Burgesses."

"More than twenty years ago. While I was in college. I needed a job to help cover my expenses, and Mrs. Burgess was looking for cheap labor. Why are you asking?"

"Please, could you sit a minute?"

Carisse hesitated for a moment, but Landon saw the minute her curiosity overtook her skepticism. She sat.

"My father was a reporter for the *Post*. He was killed twenty years ago while, I have reason to believe, looking into a story concerning Ambassador Burgess."

"Mr. Burgess was a partner at some hoity-toity law firm then."

Landon knew that. It had been easy to get background information on Burgess. The son of an oil tycoon in Texas, Burgess had gone to all the right schools from birth, including Harvard for undergraduate and law. He had accepted a job at a prominent Washington, DC law firm at graduation, working on driving policy—a polite way to say *lobbying*—for his daddy's oil company. Burgess had married his wife, an equally accomplished lawyer, who'd stopped working two years after their marriage and given him three children, two boys and a girl. The Burgesses lived a privileged life among Washington, DC's wealthy, and two years ago Burgess had been appointed to his ambassadorship. It was said he had his eye on higher office, not for himself but for his oldest son, William Burgess Junior, who had followed in his father's footsteps and become a partner at Daddy's law firm.

"Can you tell me what you remember about working for the Burgesses?"

Carisse sighed. "You're a reporter, so I guess you know why I got fired."

That had taken a little more digging, but Landon had eventually determined that Mrs. Burgess had accused Carisse of stealing a necklace.

"It was a stupid mistake, and if I could take it back, I would. School was just so expensive. I didn't have any help, and the Burgesses had so much. At the time I thought…" She shrugged. "I guess I didn't think. Mrs. Burgess confronted me the day after I took the necklace, and I fessed up and gave it back right away. That's the only reason she didn't report me to the cops, but of course, she fired me on the spot. Can't say I blame her. I'd do the same thing if I caught one of my employees stealing from me." She glanced at the counter where the line of customers was being helped.

"How long did you work for the Burgesses?" Landon asked.

"About five months. I wasn't a very good housekeeper. The Burgesses had several, two to three for each floor—if you can believe it. But the house, if you can call it that, it was more like a palace. It was huge. I only worked three days a week, helping the full-timers." Carisse looked as if she was recalling a memory. "I remember not long after I started, I accidentally broke a lamp. It was an ugly, ornate-looking thing, so you know it was expensive. I thought I was going to be fired right then and there, but the head housekeeper didn't even bat an eye. She just went into the basement storage area and came back with an exact replica of the lamp I had broken. Who keeps spare matching lamps in storage like toilet paper or soap? Rich people, that's who."

Landon wondered what the head housekeeper had been through to get to the point where she kept spare lamps on hand, but that was a question for another time.

"It wasn't exactly clear why my father was looking into Ambassador Burgess, but there was another name in his journal." Landon hesitated. Anyone living in Washington, DC, twenty years ago would have known the name *Addison Kober*. She was fifteen when she went missing. Her family had not achieved the same status as the Burgesses, but they'd been upper-middle class—the father a surgeon, the mother a successful Realtor. And Allison had made a picture-perfect victim for the media. A blonde, blue-eyed cheerleader with a smile that lit up the camera. Her disappearance had dominated the airwaves for weeks, Landon recalled. Eventually, the story had faded from the public eye, but Addison had never been found dead or alive.

"The other name in my dad's journal was *Addison Kober*."

Carisse's expression went from confusion to recognition in a couple of seconds. "The missing girl?"

Landon nodded. "Do you know if the Burgesses knew Addison or anyone in her family?"

Carisse shook her head. "I don't. I'm sure I would've remembered if I'd seen her at the house or heard her mentioned. Especially with all the media attention about her going missing. Wow, I feel bad. I'd forgotten about that poor girl. They never found her, did they?"

"No, no, they didn't," Landon confirmed.

Carisse tsked. "That's too bad I have a son now. He's four, and if anything like that ever happened to him…"

She didn't finish the statement, but she didn't have to. Their child going missing was every parent's nightmare.

Landon asked a few more questions trying to pry loose from Carisse's memory anything that might explain his father's notes, but either Carisse knew nothing that could help them, or he just didn't have enough information to hit upon the right questions to pull the answers from her memory. After a while, Carisse stood, announcing that she had to get back to work.

Landon had lost his appetite. He wrapped his sandwich in a napkin and took his root beer to go. It looked like he was going to have to dig deeper to figure out what exactly his father had been doing that had gotten him murdered.

JOHN LEONARD, Michelle's boss and owner of the Leonard Gallery, sat behind his desk in his small, cramped office. Leonard hadn't done a thing to make the space feel welcoming. The walls were bare despite the assortment of artwork just outside the door. The space was a mess, with files overflowing Leonard's desk and the small round table in the corner. A leather sofa was wedged into a corner, but it, too, was covered in files that looked like art catalogs and other papers. Leonard had gone out of the office and dug up a single folding chair, which Dora took. Logan stood at her side, making her regret sitting. It felt as if he was in charge of the interview.

Leonard had already heard about Michelle's murder and after a round of "Unbelievable" and "Can't be happening," Dora had finally gotten him to focus on her questions, although he did appear unusually anxious. It could have been nothing, but her instincts weren't leading her in that direction.

"How long have you known Ms. Quitoni?" Dora asked.

"Just since she started working here two years ago. She came highly recommended. Had both art and business experience and was from the area. It seemed like a perfect fit."

"Seemed like?" Logan said, pouncing on the equivocation.

Leonard folded his hands on the desk, then unfolded them and folded them again. "It was. It was a perfect fit."

"Has Michelle had any trouble with anyone in particular? Maybe a buyer—"

"Client." Leonard's back straightened. "We call the people that honor us by purchasing from us *clients*."

Dora gave him a tight smile. "Oh, sorry. Had there been any clients that Michelle had difficulty with? Maybe one that showed her too much or unwanted attention?"

Leonard frowned. "No. Absolutely not. I wouldn't have stood for it."

"That's an interesting way to phrase that." Logan cocked his head to the side, drawing Leonard's full attention to him. "You wouldn't have stood for it. Why? What would you have done, Mr. Leonard?"

"I... I just mean that I'm the owner. Michelle's boss. Ultimately, I'm responsible for her safety while she is within these walls. I wouldn't have tolerated a client harassing her."

"So, there was never a client that asked Michelle out for coffee or anything?" Dora pressed.

"No," Leonard said vehemently. "Fraternizing with the clients is not permitted."

Dora didn't look over at Logan, but she could feel him vibrating with the same excitement she felt. They just had to dig it out of Leonard. "Well, I can understand why you might have the rule, but come on, Mr. Leonard. Michelle is a beautiful young woman, and I'm sure a lot of the men that come in here are pretty well off. That can be attractive."

"Michelle wouldn't do that." Leonard was nearly yelling.

Dora studied the gallery owner, sure now that Eisha Steele was right about the affair between Michelle and her boss. Now she just needed Leonard to confirm it. "Why wouldn't a young woman accept a date from a handsome, wealthy man?"

Logan shot her a quick look. She was goading Leonard, but he was on the cusp of cracking.

Possibly realizing his reaction to the question had been over-the-top, Leonard stiffened. He smoothed his tie, visibly setting his expression to neutral. "I... It's not. I just meant Michelle wasn't the kind of young woman that dated around."

"We aren't here to upset you, Mr. Leonard."

"I've just found out my assistant manager was murdered. This whole situation is upsetting."

"Especially since you were having an affair with her. That must make it even more upsetting."

Leonard's cheeks were mottled with color. "I can't... That you'd even suggest... I'm a married man... I..."

Dora held up a hand to stop the sputtering man. "Mr. Leonard, I have no intention of embarrassing you or passing judgment. But I am going to get to the truth and find the man who took Michelle's life. And right now, I have to tell you, your lack of cooperation is doing you no favors."

Leonard visibly deflated. "If my wife finds out..."

"Of course we'll do our best to be discreet," Logan jumped in, with a chummy one guy to another smirk. "We only care about finding the murderer."

Leonard dropped his gaze to the desktop. "We had been having an affair. Michelle broke it off a couple weeks ago."

Dora's instincts buzzed. "Michelle broke it off?"

Leonard stiffened. "If you are suggesting that I would— Maybe I need to consult a lawyer before speaking to you further."

"That is your prerogative. If you could call your lawyer now and have him meet you down at the station...?" Dora started to stand.

Leonard swallowed hard. "Now? I... I can't just leave the gallery."

"Well, I'm sorry," Logan said, all traces of friendliness gone from his voice. "If you won't talk to us here, you'll have to speak to us at the station. With your lawyer, of course."

"Okay, okay, wait. I'll answer your questions."

Dora reclaimed her chair. "So, as you were saying, Michelle broke things off a few weeks ago."

"Yes," Leonard spat. "She wanted me to end my marriage. She was tired of sneaking around. I couldn't do that."

Breaking things off might have made Leonard angry enough to stalk Michelle. He'd certainly have the opportunity knowing her work schedule and all. "Have you been following Michelle? Stalking her?"

"What? No! I wouldn't. Look, I didn't want the thing with Michelle to end, but I couldn't leave my wife. She would have taken half of everything. The house. This gallery. I've worked too hard to lose it."

Dora disliked John Leonard more with each passing minute.

"So, your wife doesn't know about your affair?"

The look of horror on the man's face could not have been faked. "No. No. And I don't want her to. It was a stupid mistake." He turned to look at Logan pleadingly. "You can't ruin my life over a mistake."

The way Dora saw it, it was Leonard who'd ruined his own life. She had no sympathy for cheaters. And if Leonard's wife knew about the affair, she had a motive to want Michelle dead, although she doubted the woman would kill two other innocent women. But she could have killed her husband's mistress and left a trail, making it look like a serial killer was responsible. But that wasn't what Dora's gut was saying. It was saying that as much as she didn't like Leonard, he nor his wife had anything to do with Michelle's death. Still, she'd have to speak to Mrs. Leonard. If that put John in a bad spot, well, it was no less than he deserved for his actions.

"Mr. Leonard, where were you between nine p.m. Friday night and six a.m. Monday morning?"

Leonard let his head fall into his hands. "I can't believe this."

"Mr. Leonard, please answer my question."

"Friday night I was home with my wife and kids all night. I got home around six, and I was with them all week-end. I left for work around seven thirty Monday morning." He lifted his head. "Are we done?"

"For now," Dora said. She and Logan rose and went to the office door. At the door, she turned back. "You know, Mr. Leonard, in my experience, the truth has a way of coming out. It might be better for you if your wife heard the truth from you before it does."

"It's looking more and more like Michelle Quitoni wasn't the perfect senator's daughter that her parents wanted everyone to believe she was," Logan said once they'd gotten back into the car and were headed out of the parking lot.

"No, she wasn't." Dora agreed. "But I don't know if any of it has anything to do with her murder. I don't see how anything we've learned really helps us. We'll look into whether Leonard might have had something to do with the murder, but my gut is saying no."

She was sure that Michelle was the victim of the serial killer currently stalking Washington, DC's streets, but she had to cover all her bases. It was possible that Michelle had known her killer and that he or she had patterned the murder to look like the other two murders that had been in the news. Possible, but not likely in Dora's professional opinion.

"My gut is saying 'Feed me,'" Logan said, pulling her back into the conversation she'd been having with him before her thoughts wandered. "We haven't had lunch. How about stopping some place?"

Dora shot him a look as she made a right turn onto Georgia Avenue.

"What? We both have to eat."

"Fine. Do you have any particular place in mind?"

Logan grinned. "I do know a place, and it's not that far."

Chapter Fourteen

Logan was thrilled that Dora had accepted his invitation to lunch. Maybe with time, she would see her way to forgiving him. Maybe even giving him a second chance. It was a long shot, maybe the longest shot he'd ever taken, but he knew he had to take it. He'd been wrong to run away from what they'd had, and he was ready to atone for that. If she let him. That, he knew, was still an open question.

He directed her to a seafood restaurant on Water Street in the Southwest Waterfront neighborhood of DC. The neighborhood had seen an economic boom over the last decade, with restaurants, bars, and posh hotels popping up along the mile long stretch of land fronting the Potomac River. It had bought new life to the iconic area, but the downside had been an increase in the cost of living in the area pushing out many of the older, longer time residents.

Whaler's Seafood had survived the changing times, remaining family owned, and Logan did his best to support it, eating there at least once a week. He'd discovered the restaurant not long after moving back to the city. It was new, but the chef knew his business. As far as Logan was concerned, there wasn't better calamari in the city and the blackened swordfish was awe-inspiring.

Once seated at a table by the window, he ordered the

calamari for him and Dora to share and the swordfish for his entrée.

"May as well go big since the FBI is paying," Dora said with a playful grin on her face.

Logan laughed. "Order whatever you want. It's on me."

Somehow, talking about the case in such a nice restaurant didn't feel appropriate. Or maybe they both just needed a break. In any case, the conversation moved in the direction of two old colleagues catching up. He told her about Arizona and the FBI, caught her up on his sister, Lisa's, life post-divorce, and Landon's travels all over the world as an investigative reporter.

"And what about you? Anyone special in your life?" Dora asked.

He couldn't tell from her inflection if she was just making idle chitchat or if there was a more personal reason for her question, though he hoped it was the latter.

"No wife. No girlfriend. No one special." Was that relief he saw on her face, or was it just wishful thinking on his part? "I haven't seen anyone seriously since we broke up."

"It wasn't really a breakup, though, right?" Dora said. "I mean, we weren't serious, as it turned out."

"Dora, I'm sorry if I made you feel that way. I do value our relationship. I still do."

She brought the water to her lips and looked away. "Maybe we should talk about something else."

"What if I don't want to talk about something else?" Then, to lighten the tone, he added, "I told you my relationship status. It's only fair you tell me yours."

Dora sighed. "Single," she said, cutting into her steak. "The last guy I was seeing decided to go back to his former girlfriend." She flinched, and he wondered if that meant she'd cared for him or that she still did. "It wasn't serious," she said, almost as if she had read his mind. "We'd only been seeing each other for a few weeks. It seems as if I have a type. Men who don't stick."

"That guy was an idiot."

Dora shot him a look. "There are a lot of idiots out there."

Logan set his fork down and pushed his plate to the side. "I know you don't want to hear this, but you're right. I was an idiot. Instead of talking to you about what I was feeling, about the grief over losing my mother, I shut down and closed myself off to you and to my family. I made drastic changes to my life—some good, others I deeply regret."

"You don't have to—"

"Yes, I do. I have to say that I'm sorry I hurt you. And I miss you. I want to make it up to you and prove I can be the man you deserve. I want to try again." There. He'd said it.

He reached across the table and covered her hand with his. His heart leapt when she let him. He held her in a heated gaze that they didn't break off until the waiter came back to check on them.

Dora moved her hand from under his. "I think we should focus on the case," she said, reaching for her water again.

"And after the case?"

She didn't answer. They ate the rest of their lunch in silence. Logan paid the bill, and they made their way out of the restaurant and back to the car.

He stopped at the driver's-side door beside Dora. "I don't want to upset you, but I want to be clear that I meant what I said. I want a second chance for us, and I'll do whatever you need me to do to prove it."

"I don't know if you can," Dora said softly.

He brought his hand to her cheek and gazed into her eyes. "Will you let me try?"

The seconds ticked by, but Dora finally nodded and the knot in his chest unraveled. He bent his head to kiss her, but her phone trilled before he had a chance to taste her lips.

Dora stepped back and pulled her phone from her purse. "Madison." She listened to whatever was being said on the other end of the phone, a smile slowly blowing across her face. "That's great work, Roberts. Text me the address, will you? Logan and I will go check it out."

"What's up?" Logan asked back in FBI mode, even though the thought of their almost kiss lingered in his mind.

"Roberts found a flower shop in Arlington that recently sold several desert roses."

Logan felt a smile that matched Dora's smile spread across his face. "Sounds like a lead to me. Let's go check it out."

A TALL, MUSCLED Black man in his thirties stood behind the counter of the flower shop. He had a round face, dark brown eyes, and black locs pulled back in a bun at the nape of his neck. He wore a green apron over a gray T-shirt and jeans. He finished ringing up the purchases of a young man before turning to Logan and Dora.

"How can I help you?" he asked in a friendly voice.

Dora and Logan held up their identification. "Detective Dora Madison with the DC Metropolitan Police Department. And this is Logan Elkins with the FBI. Are you Darice Thompson?"

"I am." His eyes narrowed. "What is this all about?"

"We're investigating the murder of several women that occurred in the city recently. We contacted Markham Blooms Wholesalers, and they mentioned that you had ordered a large quantity of desert-rose seeds about two months ago."

His features softened. "What does that have to do with a serial killer?"

"We are hoping you can clear up a few things for us," Logan said without answering Darius's question.

"I'll answer whatever questions you have. I don't have anything to hide." Darius held his hands up, palms out, as if to emphasize his statement.

"So, about these desert-rose seeds."

"Oh, yeah, well, obviously, we order a lot of seeds." He gestured to the flower shop.

"The wholesaler said you'd never ordered these particular kinds of seeds before," Dora shot back.

Darius's face scrunched up. "Well, no, let me take a look in our system." He turned to the computer he'd used moments before to ring up the previous customer. "Two months ago, you said?"

"Approximately," Dora responded.

"Ah, here it is. Yeah, I remember this order now. It was a special order for the customer. One hundred seeds of the Never Forget You variety. Paid in cash."

Of course it was paid in cash, because nothing could ever be easy for her, Dora thought.

"Never forget you?" Logan said.

"Well, that's what some people call this particular color of the flower. Because of the deep purple color at the tips of the pink petals, some people interpret it as a little bit of sadness amongst the brightness. They are often sent to people who have just suffered a loss." Darius shrugged.

Logan shot Dora a look that told her he was thinking along the same lines as her. Was it a message of some sort from the killer to his victims? That he would never forget them?

"Does the customer on that order have a name?" Dora asked.

"John Smith." Darius cringed, possibly realizing what Dora instinctively knew. The name *John Smith* was undoubtedly an alias.

"What about a phone number?" Logan asked.

"Yeah, yeah, right here." Darius rattled off the number, and Dora took it down in her notebook.

"Would you mind making me a copy of what you have there, Mr. Thompson?"

"No problem. Anything I can do to help." He hit a couple buttons on the keyboard, and a few seconds later, the printer behind him whirled to life. He passed the still warm sheet of paper to Dora. "Anything else I can do for you, Officers?"

Dora ignored being called Officer. She'd learned long ago that most people didn't mean it as a slight. They just saw all law enforcement the same. Officers, detectives, FBI agents—they were all just cops to the general public.

"You could tell us where you were Friday evening through Monday morning."

Darius his eyes went wide. "I am…" He stopped, then started again, giving a detailed accounting of his whereabouts for the time period.

Even though Randi had identified the man she saw leaving Michelle in the park as a white man, Dora had to make sure she had all her bases covered. Darius had access to the seeds, and the customer's name was an obvious fake. Maybe he was working with a partner. It was unlikely, but she wasn't willing to leave any stone unturned.

She showed Darius a photo of the sketch of their suspect on her phone. "Do you recognize this man? Could he be the person who ordered the seeds?"

Darius studied the phone screen for several long moments before shaking his head. "Sorry. We get a lot of people in here, and it was two months ago."

Dora and Logan thanked him and then headed back to the car.

"Mr. Smith is our guy," Logan said when they were back in the car.

"Yeah." Dora started the engine. "But who is he?"

Chapter Fifteen

Logan stood next to Dora, both of them under the glaring sunlight, watching the activity around the crime scene. Another woman was dead. Senselessly murdered by a madman. He could feel the rage, frustration, and, yes, despair rolling off Dora in waves. If she didn't learn to compartmentalize, she wasn't going to make it in this career. She'd been visibly angry since they'd gotten the call that another woman's body had been found. He was going to have to find a way to force Dora to get some rest and unwind, but he knew that wouldn't be easy as long as this killer was on the loose.

He focused his attention back on the crime scene in front of him. The similarity to the previous scenes was jarring. The woman had been found posed with a desert rose in her hair and the words *Protect the innocent* written on her left side. She'd been strangled, just like the killer's other victims. The one difference: The victim hadn't been found for several days. The killer must not have known that the area of the park that he left the body in was closed to foot traffic or maintenance on a crumbling walking path. The woman hadn't been found until a work crew had arrived to complete the work.

"Who are you?" Dora mumbled.

They hadn't found any identification, at least not yet. Logan wasn't sure the question was directed at the killer or their victim, but from the intensity with which Dora gazed at the medical examiner and his assistant as they hunched over the body, he guessed the latter. "We will figure out who she is and make sure whoever did this to her is brought to justice."

Dora didn't respond. Instead, she headed for the medical examiner's side. "What can you tell me, Dean?"

"Not a whole lot yet," Dean said. "I'm ready to move her to my office. I'll get started on the autopsy right away. We need to catch this monster."

"From your lips," Logan said.

Dean stood to his full height. "I can tell you that she fought him. Hard. I've got bruises on her arms and legs and chipped fingernails."

"DNA?" Logan asked.

"Possibly, but I'd need something to match it to unless we get lucky, and our guy is already in the system."

They wouldn't get that lucky; Logan was sure of that. But if Dean found DNA this time, they'd at least have some hard evidence when they had a suspect in custody.

"I'm pretty sure she died by strangulation, based on the bruising around her neck, and her hyoid bone is fractured."

The DNA. The dumpsite that had been closed. Their killer was getting sloppy. Was the attention getting to him? Or was it something else? And more importantly, how would it change his behavior? One thing that profiling counted on was a killer's consistency. If their killer was unraveling… Who knew what that meant or their investigation. Or future victims.

"How about an estimate on time of death?" Dora asked Dean, bringing Logan's focus back to the moment.

"Well, she's been exposed to the elements for at least twenty-four hours, based on the decomposition and rigor, but thankfully, the cold has preserved a lot."

Yes, thankfully. A small shiver snaked its way down Logan's spine. Medical examiners were necessary, but he could have never done the job himself.

Dean motioned for his assistant.

Logan was following Dora back to the car when his phone rang.

He answered while he was walking.

"Where are you?" Kaj's voice rang excitedly over the line. "I've got something for you from the video."

"We're on our way."

They made the drive to Kaj's office in record time.

Kaj was waiting for them in his office when they arrived.

"Finally!" he said.

"I'm here. Finally."

"Okay, what's on this video that's got you so worked up?" Dora stepped over to the desk.

Logan stood behind her.

"I got you a clear shot of your guy." Kaj opened the laptop and pressed the space bar.

Grainy black-and-white footage played on the laptop screen. The front yard of a house similar to Michelle's was visible. A car drove past.

Logan glanced away from the screen at Kaj. "I hope it gets more exciting than this."

"Just wait for it." He was practically vibrating.

Ten more seconds passed, and another car came into the frame. This time, the car stopped at the curb in front of the house and a man got out of the driver's side. It was late, but the streetlights provided enough light to illuminate the man's face.

Logan leaned forward in his chair. "That's—"

"Leonard," Dora interrupted with a hard grimace. "And check the date-time stamp."

Saturday, August 12, 2:07 a.m. The night Michelle went missing.

Logan's pulse quickened. "Where exactly was this video taken?"

"Keene said he got it from a neighbor three blocks north of Michelle's house."

Three blocks.

Leonard was three blocks away during the time frame when Michelle went missing. That couldn't be a coincidence.

"Rewind it," Logan ordered. His heart was pumping so fast that he had to take slow deep breaths to try and slow his breathing while he watched the video a second time.

Kaj dragged his finger over the mouse, and the vehicle pulled up again with Leonard's car coming to a stop at the curb once again.

There wasn't much to it. Leonard got out of the car, looked both ways down the street, then disappeared around the side of the house. He was dressed in all black—black jeans, a top, even black boots. Which alone didn't mean much, but the flinty look he shot up and down the street was more than just a little suspicious. As was the fact that he parked three blocks from Michelle's house. It might have just been because the two were having an affair and he didn't want his car to be seen in her driveway at that hour. But that didn't explain why Leonard hadn't mentioned this little trip when he and Dora had questioned him.

"We need to bring Leonard in right now," Logan barked.

"Agreed," Dora said, already pulling out her phone. "But I don't know. Does this feel too easy to you?"

"I wouldn't call anything about this case easy," Logan responded. "But this video puts Leonard at Michelle's house on the night she went missing. Making him potentially the last person to see her alive. And he lied to us—or at least he didn't tell us about it."

Dora punched the screen on her phone as she headed for the office door. "Let's go see what Mr. Leonard has to say for himself."

Twenty minutes later, Logan pulled to a stop in front of a modest two-story house where John Leonard lived with his wife, Felicia. The grass in the front yard could have used a cut, but the house looked well-kept and loved. The home was in the expensive Chevy Chase neighborhood, so the Leonards weren't doing too badly for themselves.

Dora pointed to the colorful flower beds on either side of the main door. "Someone likes to garden."

Logan leaned over her, peering out of the passenger side window.

She breathed in the scent of his spicy, masculine cologne. Thankfully, he didn't seem to notice.

"Interesting, although I don't see any blooms that look like our desert rose."

"No," Dora agreed, grateful when Logan sat back in the driver's seat, to temper the effects he'd been having on her body. "But it may be worth asking a few questions of Leonard about his garden."

Logan shot her a smile before they both got out of the car.

Rain had been threatening for days, and the dark gray clouds floating across the sky promised to make good on the threat sooner rather than later. She could only hope they were back at the station by then.

"What do we know about the wife?" Logan asked as they made their way to the front door.

"She's thirty-two. A nurse. No criminal record." Dora repeated what she knew about Felicia Leonard, which wasn't much. Neither of the Leonards had criminal records. But that didn't mean John Leonard wasn't their guy. It just meant he'd never been caught.

She and Logan climbed the stairs of the wide porch and flanked the door before knocking. Seconds turned into a full minute, and when no one responded, Dora knocked again.

"No one home?" Logan said.

"Maybe," Dora responded, but her senses were tingling. She tried to see inside through the sidelights next to the door, but the frost was too heavy to detect any movement.

She pressed her ear to the door and heard the sound of someone moving inside. "There's someone in there."

She knocked again harder, the sound almost blocking out the sound of another door opening.

"He's running," Logan said, already moving down the porch stairs.

Dora followed him. They rounded the side of the house.

Leonard was already behind the wheel of a black Mercedes. He looked up, fear and determination hardening the planes of his face.

Dora held up her badge with one hand, the other poised on the butt of her gun. "Police. Freeze!"

Leonard started the car's engine and hit the gas.

Dora leapt out of the way but not before the side of the car clipped her. She hit the grassy lawn face-first. She flipped over.

"Are you okay?" Logan ran at her from the other side of the driveway, where he'd darted out of the way of the Mercedes.

Her hip throbbed where the Mercedes nicked her. "Yeah, I'm good."

Logan's gaze swept over her, ensuring that she was, in fact, fine. He extended a hand and pulled her to her feet. She flinched.

"You need medical attention."

"I need to catch this guy."

The Mercedes sped down the residential street.

"Let's go!" Dora yelled, ignoring the pain as she ran back toward the car.

Logan moved behind the wheel of the police sedan as she jumped into the car, fastening her seat belt with one hand as he wheeled away from the curb after the Mercedes.

Leonard sped up. Logan stayed with him.

Dora gripped the bar above the door tightly enough that her knuckles whitened. "He's going to get someone killed."

Luckily, they were the only two cars on the residential street at this point in the midday, but that wasn't likely to last. They were only a few blocks from the main thoroughfare, where Leonard could end up killing someone with the way he was driving.

Dora turned on the sirens and lights, then radioed their position, calling for backup.

About three car lengths ahead, Leonard careened into the intersection, turning left onto Connecticut Avenue, barely missing sideswiping a minivan.

"Damnit," Logan followed, slowing his pace slightly.

Leonard jerked the Camaro onto the wrong side of the road. Horns blared.

"He's going to get himself killed!" Dora exclaimed.

The Mercedes rocketed to the front of the line of traffic. The cars in front of Dora and Logan responded much more slowly to the sound of their sirens.

"We're losing him!" Dora yelled.

"I can see that, but there's nothing I can do unless you want me to drive as recklessly as Leonard."

They heard the crash before they saw it.

The Mercedes had swerved into oncoming traffic again. Only Leonard misjudged the amount of space he had to get back on the right side of the road. He slammed head on into the back of a box truck, knocking the Mercedes into and then over the curb.

Pedestrians scattered, and Dora said a quick thank-you to the gods that none of them seemed to have been hit. The Mercedes had been moving fast enough that jumping the curb didn't slow it much at all. It kept moving forward, right into a low brick wall that surrounded a parking lot.

Tires screeched as drivers came to abrupt stops on the street and screams filled the air.

Logan punched the brake, stopping the car in the middle of the street. They both threw their doors open and ran for the wreck.

The front of the car had folded like an accordion.

People drew forward, many of them with their cameras out and recording.

Dora silently cursed them. She reached through the shattered driver's-side window and pressed two fingers against the side of Leonard's neck. There was a pulse—a faint one, but it was there.

"He's alive." Dora pulled her hand back. "Call for an ambulance."

Logan pulled out his phone and made the call.

They'd have to wait for the EMTs to get Leonard out of the car. It was too dangerous to move him.

Dora's legs gave out, and she went down onto her knee. It was then that she realized that she was bleeding as well.

"Dora!" Logan was beside her in an instant.

She pressed a hand to her side and pulled it back bloody.

"You're hurt. I'm going to call for another ambulance," Logan pronounced, fear lacing his words.

She had no desire to go to the hospital and was just about to tell him that when a wave of dizziness hit her. "I think that's probably a good idea."

Chapter Sixteen

John Leonard had survived surgery, but he was in critical condition. Logan was happy to hear it. Hopefully, Leonard would be able to answer some questions soon. He and Dora had plenty of them for him.

Luckily, Dora's injury was minor. Her bleeding at the scene of the accident had come from a scratch on her side. The emergency room doctor theorized that the wave of dizziness had resulted from an adrenaline crash. He'd discharged her with orders to take ibuprofen if her side bothered her and to take it easy. She took the ibuprofen without argument but taking it easy was a different story. Keene, Roberts, and Crenshaw had put in appearances at the hospital while he'd waited for Dora to be discharged.

The hours waiting at the hospital had also given Logan a chance to check in with his colleagues at the FBI. He was surprised to find out that John Leonard wasn't unknown to the Bureau. In fact, he was the subject of an ongoing investigation into money laundering. Logan had to wonder if Leonard running from them had more to do with that than their serial killer case. Leonard didn't exactly fit the profile he was working up on their serial killer. But all those questions would have to wait until Leonard regained consciousness.

After four hours at the hospital, Dora's doctor finally discharged her. Logan had the foresight to get Landon to drop off his personal vehicle so that he could drive Dora home. He led Dora into her house. "Are you hungry?" he asked. He knew he was. He hadn't wanted to leave Dora to find the hospital's cafeteria, so he'd had to make do with a bag of stale chips from the vending machine.

Dora stopped him from trekking to the fridge with a hand on his arm. "I don't want food."

Heat filled her eyes. She brought her lips to his gently.

The surprise that flooded through him quickly changed to desire. He forced himself to pull back, though. "Dora, wait. I'm not sure you're thinking this through."

"I don't want to think right now. I want to feel. We could have been killed today."

He rested his hands on her waist. "I don't want you to regret anything."

"No regrets," she promised.

Logan turned his face into her hand, his lips brushing her palm. His feelings churned through him even as he reminded himself that this was real. Dora was really in his arms.

A moment later, she stretched up on her toes and brushed her lips over his.

When she pulled back, he searched her face and saw joy, awe, and fear—all the same feelings that were swirling inside of him. He wrapped his arms around her, pulling her against his chest, and kissed her with everything he was feeling.

Dora groaned against his lips and snaked her fingers around his neck.

"Let me stay the night," Logan panted against her lips.

"Please." He didn't care about the desperation in his voice. He simply knew he needed to be with Dora.

A smile stretched across Dora's face, and she nodded, drawing him in for another kiss before leading her through to the back of the small house where her bedroom was located. He moved to her toward the bed, cupping her cheeks. He kissed her deeply. He hadn't realized how desperately he missed her kiss. He missed the way her lips moved against his and the smell of her floral perfume circling around him.

He stopped bedside, his hands moving to the buttons of her shirt and undoing each in turn, baring her chest to the cool air. His body warmed as the blouse slid from her shoulders onto the floor. He stepped back from her, his eyes roved her body. Her cheeks pinked.

"You are beautiful," he whispered.

Dora unclasped the buttons on her slacks and let them slide down her legs before reaching around her back and unsnapping her bra. It hit the floor only seconds before her panties, and he thought his heart might actually stop. She let him look his fill for several long moments before stepping into him. He reached a hand around her waist, tucking his head into her shoulder and stroking his tongue over the spot on her neck in the way he remembered she loved.

Her body trembled, and Logan held her tighter to him. He let his hand drift lower until it skimmed the apex of her thighs. The contact made her gasp in a little breath. He smiled into her neck as he lavished it with kisses. He slid his finger over the sensitive nerves between her legs, eliciting another moan from her. Her head fell onto his shoulder.

"Logan, I can't. It's too much."

"Just relax. I've got you." There was nothing he wanted more in life at that moment than to bring her to her release.

His hand worked between her thighs while his lips continued to caress her neck.

Dora's breath came in quick pants now, and he knew she was close. He snaked his free hand from around her waist and to her breast. He twirled his finger over her nipple, drawing another moan from her. He curled the finger inside of her and built up speed, drawing another moan from her even as he felt her tightening around his fingers. Her moan turned into a cry, and her body spasmed. He moved his arm back around her waist, holding her up as he wrung every drop of pleasure from her. When she finally went limp in his arms, he laid her across the bed and quickly disposed of his own clothes.

Desire still coursed through his veins. He wasn't anywhere near done with the pleasure he planned for both of them to enjoy that night. He wasn't sure he'd ever tire of exploring her body. He removed his trousers, kicking them away without his eyes leaving her face.

"I want you. So much," he said, climbing onto the bed and stretching out over her.

His mouth collided with hers in a claiming kiss. His manhood pressed against her stomach. He felt his body harden against her belly. He hovered over her, his manhood nudging at her entrance. They stared at each other as he pushed into her, moving slowly at first, her body opening to him and stretching to accommodate him. Each inch filled his own heart with more of her until he was sure it would burst. When he was fully seated, he stilled. It wasn't the right time to say it, but he knew, without a doubt, this... this was right. This, Dora was everything, and he loved her. Had loved her from almost the moment they met.

Then she reached up, cupping his cheek, drawing him in even deeper, and his control shattered. He moved faster, each thrust leading to her making little mewling sounds that only drove his desire higher. She clutched at his backside, demanding his hips move faster and harder.

"Does it feel good to have me inside of you again?" Logan growled against her lips.

"Yes," she panted. "God, yes."

Her affirmation drove him closer to his release. He thrust into her, saying with his body what he wasn't yet ready to say with his words. She broke. His lips collided with hers, swallowing her moans of ecstasy as she continued to writhe beneath him. His last driving thrusts pushed him over the edge, and he moaned her name as he followed her over the cliff. They toppled over and over, shattering before coming back together. Together.

It was the first time in a long time that he'd felt whole.

They lay in each other's arms, not speaking, just holding each other, being together until Dora's breathing evened out. She hadn't asked him to leave, so he pulled her in closer and let his body relax into sleep, wondering if he just might get lucky and convince her to end every night just like this for the rest of their lives.

DORA WOKE WITH what felt like a boulder on her chest. Logan's warm breath tickled her ear. She slid from under the weight of his arm.

His eyes fluttered open. "Hey, where are you going?"

She hastily threw on her undergarments and slid into her jeans. She did a full three-hundred-sixty-degree turn looking for her shirt. "I have to go...you have to go."

Logan sat up in the bed, his mouth turning into a frown. "Dora?"

This had been a mistake. A huge mistake. She'd clearly learned nothing from their past. Not to mention that they were working together again. What was it they said about fools making the same mistakes over and over? Clearly, she was such a fool.

"Listen, we need to get into the station. There's a lot to do today. I know you probably want to go home to shower and change before going in, so I ordered an Uber. It should be here in a few minutes."

She left the room without giving him a chance to respond.

She made coffee, continuing to chastise herself as she did. *God, how stupid do you have to be to fall into bed with the man who broke your heart?*

Logan padded into the kitchen fully dressed but without his shoes. "So, we're not going to talk about it?"

The coffee maker hissed before the brown liquid began dripping into the carafe.

"There's nothing to talk about," Dora said, not daring to look at him. "It was a mistake. It won't happen again. No one needs to know."

"I know. You know."

She did look at him now, and she let her anger fuel her. "Logan, I am not going down this road with you again. It was just sex. That's all it can be."

"That's all you wanted to be, but that's not all it was. I think you know that."

Dora frowned. "Let's not do this."

"Do what, Dora? Care about each other?"

She threw up her hands. "Fall into this trap of thinking that this time things are going to be different."

"They can be different this time. Our relationship ended because I had to move to Arizona for work."

"Is that why it ended, though? I mean, we could have tried the long-distance thing. I offered to try, and you said no."

"Long distance is—"

She moved in closer to him, crowding him. "Is what, Logan? People do it. People who really want to be together. People who are committed to trying. That was our problem. Not the distance. Not the jobs. You weren't committed to us."

She looked into his eyes, waiting for an answer. Waiting for him to tell her she was wrong, but he seemed to be struggling with the ability to speak.

"Nothing? Really." She shook her head. "Last night was...was great, but it was last night. A onetime thing. I'd like to keep it that way." She unplugged the coffee machine. "My car should be outside. I'll see you later."

She brushed past him, grabbing her purse, and left the kitchen without another word.

"The witness couldn't describe the man she saw. Not in any detail." The killer listened to the two officers talking to one another, leaning forward, ignoring the pounding of his heart. He had to stay calm and not look as if he were eavesdropping even though he was. No one in the police station paid him much attention. It was one of his gifts. He looked as if he belonged no matter where he was. So, nobody noticed when he stopped abruptly, having overheard the officers talking at their desks. He needed to get as much information as possible about this witness.

"Detective Madison has her holed up somewhere supersecret. She's hoping once the witness feels safe, she will be able to give the task force more details about the man she saw."

"It's possible," the other cop responded.

The first nodded. "Let's hope so. We really need to

catch this monster." One of the officers' phones rang, ending their conversation.

There was a witness, but she hadn't given the police anything. Yet.

He had to find her before she did. He needed more time to find his Sarah.

Detective Madison. The cops had said Madison had stashed the witness somewhere safe. Which meant Madison was the key.

He had to be careful, but if he followed Madison, she'd eventually lead him to the witness. And then he'd take care of her, just like he'd taken care of the others.

Chapter Seventeen

Monica Gonzalez, their first victim, had been found in a park in the trendy Foggy Bottom neighborhood, making the case a Metropolitan Police case. But her parents lived in Wheaton, Maryland, a middle-class suburb about ten miles north of DC. It was a diverse community with good schools and an abundance of single-family homes. The kind of place parents moved to give their kids the best start they could in life. But as the Gonzalezes had tragically discovered, no neighborhood was completely safe from life's dangers.

"Monica had gotten her life back on track," Lupe Gonzalez insisted. Mrs. Gonzalez taught third grade, which undoubtedly meant she was made of stern stuff. But her hands shook as she brought the coffee, she'd insisted on making for them to her lips. Dr. Gonzalez placed a meaty hand on his wife's shoulder and squeezed. When Dora had called to ask if she and Logan could drop by to speak with the couple, Mrs. Gonzalez had agreed but said her husband was at work at his dentistry practice. Robert Gonzalez must have canceled his afternoon appointments after his wife's call and come straight home because he answered the door of their brick rambler when Dora and Logan rang the bell.

"She was an all-state runner," Mrs. Gonzalez continued.

"Did you know that? In high school. We were so proud. She went to College Park," the woman continued, using the shorthand for the University of Maryland's flagship campus. "Monica wanted to be a doctor, but then she met Augustine." Mrs. Gonzalez said the name as if it was an epithet.

"Augustine Salerno." Dr. Gonzalez picked up the narrative with only slightly less disgust in his tone. "Monica was enchanted. She focused so much on track and her grades in high school. I think this was her first taste of puppy love and it was overwhelming for her." Dr. Gonzalez's eyes filled with tears.

"I could tell he was no good from the start. He'd been in school for four years when Monica met him and still wasn't anywhere close to graduating. I told Monica she should stay away from him. But she thought she could help him. Save him, you know what I mean?" Mrs. Gonzalez's eyes bore into Dora's.

She did know what the woman meant. Monica wasn't the first and she wouldn't be the last woman to give her best trying to save a man who didn't want saving. But Dorothy also knew Augustine Salerno had nothing to do with Monica Gonzalez's death. She had thoroughly investigated the man right after they found Monica's body. He struggled with a drug addiction and had physically, mentally, emotionally, and financially abused Monica and several of the women who he'd been living off of. But at the time of Monica's death, he'd been in Rio de Janeiro, and there was no indication that he had contact with Monica four months prior to her death.

Still, Dora waited patiently, listening to the Gonzalezes rail about the man they blamed for their daughter's death. She knew they needed to get it out of their system before they could be able to help her investigation. If they could be of any help. That remained to be seen.

Once the Gonzalezes' rage had run cold, Dora went through the series of questions she asked them in the days right after Monica's murder, hoping time had jarred loose new details that might put them on the killer's trail. Unfortunately, the Gonzalezes' answers shed no new light on their daughter's murder or the subsequent murders.

"We've answered all these questions already," Lupe said impatiently. "How come you didn't care this much when it was just our daughter who'd been murdered? Nobody cared."

"I assure you that is not true, Mrs. Gonzalez," Logan said.

"Isn't it? I didn't see you here then, Mr. FBI Special Agent. The cops didn't care anything about our Monica. They just saw her as a druggie, even though she'd kicked her addiction by the time that monster took her from us. She'd done rehab and had been keeping up with her therapy for almost a year. But all you saw was a junkie," Lupe spat at Dora.

Dora didn't contradict the grieving mother. She knew that there was nothing she could say that would stem the hurt and anger at her loss. As she knew there was nothing, she could say that wouldn't sound like an excuse. That she hadn't known she was dealing with a serial killer at the time. That she'd gone by the book, treating Monica like every other victim. That she'd looked into any possible drug-related angle and found, as Mrs. Gonzalez said, that Monica had kicked her habit. It was all true and none of it mattered. Monica was dead, and because Dora hadn't found her killer quickly enough, two other women were also now dead.

Dora showed both the Gonzalezes the sketch of their suspect. Neither recognized the man.

Doro and Logan left the couple to try to reseal the wound they just ripped open again.

"You know she's a grieving mother and that nothing she said about your work on the case is true," Logan said as they made their way across the Gonzalezes' lawn to the car.

"No, I don't know that." Dora held up her hand to stop Logan's protest before they got started. "I know I did the best I could with the information I had at the time, but—" Dora stopped and turned to him as they reached the car. "If Monica Gonzalez had been a senator's daughter or if Michelle Quitoni had been the first victim instead of the third, would the FBI have sent you to me sooner? Would my department have put together a task force with four detectives immediately?"

Logan deflated. "Probably. Yes, they would have."

"Exactly." Dora shucked her chin in the direction of the rancher they had just left. Mrs. Gonzalez stood in the front window watching them, her arms crossed across her chest, abject grief covering her face. "And she knows that too."

DORA SPENT THE rest of the workday into the evening at her desk, poring over every bit of information they had on each of the homicides. There appeared to be little commonality among the murder victims, apart from their looks. Michelle was an investment banker, Monica Gonzalez had been a cashier, and Alicia Jones was a preschool teacher. There was no sign that the women knew each other or had ever crossed paths with each other. Logan had pointed out that the similarity in appearance between the victims showed an undeniable pattern, but there was nothing to connect the victims in any other way. And there was nothing she could find that would lead them to their killer. What was she missing? There must've been something.

Logan sat at the desk across from her, the spicy, musky scent of his cologne gently tickling her nose. Her mind wandered to the memory of their night together. She'd forgotten how Logan was in bed and how wonderful it felt to wake up beside him. A flicker of desire coursed through her, but she pushed it down as far as she could force it. Their night had been a one-time thing. She couldn't let it happen again.

She focused back on the case, continuing her search for anything, any miniscule thing, that might lead her to her serial killer.

Logan's cell phone rang, and he answered it. Dora only had to hear his end of the conversation to know that he was speaking to his sister, Lisa.

"I'm sorry I forgot about dinner. I'm at the station, but I'll leave now." Logan went silent, but his gaze skimmed over Dora. "Yes, she's here." He fell silent for another moment. "I'm not sure she'll want to."

There was another, longer silence from Logan, and then he sighed. He pulled the phone from his ear, punching the speaker button.

"Dora?" Lisa's voice came loud and clear from the other side of the phone.

"Lisa, ah, hi. How are you?"

"I'm great. How are you?"

"I'm doing well," Dora responded, shooting a look at Logan over the top of her computer monitor. He shrugged and kept holding his phone out.

"Listen, Logan is heading to my house for dinner. I'm inviting you as well."

"Oh, that is so…nice," Dora said, surprised. She hadn't

spoken to Lisa since the breakup. "I really have a lot of work to do here. I'm not sure…"

"I'm not going to take no for an answer. I haven't seen you in ages, and no matter how much work you have to do, you also have to eat."

Dora gave Logan another beseeching look that he ignored.

"So, hop in the car with Logan." Lisa bulldozed ahead. "I'll see you both in a half hour." The phone went dead.

"I could have used a little help." Dora glared at Logan.

He shrugged. "Lisa is right. You do have to eat. And you know my sister. If you aren't at her table in exactly thirty minutes, she'll just come down here with a bunch of Tupperware and feed you anyway."

That did sound like Lisa Elkins. She tended to get what she wanted. It was what made her a good attorney.

"Come on. It's just dinner. And maybe taking your mind off the case for a bit will shake something you've missed loose," Logan cajoled.

As if in agreement, her stomach grumbled. She was hungry. And, as she remembered, Lisa was an amazing cook.

"Okay, fine, but I'm taking these files home with me."

Logan shook his head. "Has anyone ever told you you're a workaholic?"

A tentative smile curled Dora's lips. "It's been mentioned a time or two."

The drive to Lisa's Takoma Park neighborhood, just south of Catholic University, took less than thirty minutes. The house hadn't changed much since the last time Dora had visited. It was a modest, brick, two-story colonial in Takoma Park, not far from the border with Maryland. A big picture window looked out onto a wide front porch and the street beyond.

Logan pulled to the curb, and they got out, walking up the tidy concrete walkway.

Logan pressed his hand to the small of Dora's back, guiding her up the steps of the front porch. He opened the front door without knocking or using a key. The sound of laughter and Alicia Keys's "Fallin'" on the radio followed them into the house as they entered.

Lisa Elkins stuck her head around the corner leading from the kitchen, a dishrag slung over her shoulder.

A smile bloomed on her face when her gaze landed on Dora. "Dora, it's good to see you."

The scent of roast beef and sweet potatoes encircled Dora as Lisa pulled her into a full-body hug.

"It's good to see you too," Dora responded against Lisa's shoulder.

"Lisa, let her breathe," Logan said, easing Dora from his sister's arms.

Lisa let go of Dora and turned back toward the kitchen, calling out, "Landon, Dora is here!"

Landon Elkins strode into the foyer. The eldest Elkins, Landon was built broader than his younger brother but exuded a quiet strength that neither of his brasher younger siblings had. All three Elkins shared the same dark brown skin, matching dark brown eyes and high cheekbones, though. No one would doubt they were siblings.

"Hey there. Long time no see, stranger." Landon pulled Dora into a quick one-armed hug.

A high-pitched teenage voice preceded the teenager it came from into the foyer. "What's going on? I thought we were about to eat. Oh!" The teenage girl stopped short.

It had been years since Dora had seen Layla Williamson. The young girl had grown into quite a beauty.

"Hi, Layla. I'm Dora. We met, but you probably don't remember me."

"Yeah, I do remember, kind of. Hi. Can we eat now?"

Lisa rolled her eyes at her daughter but moved back toward the kitchen. "We can sit down. The food is ready."

The group trooped into the dining room where the table had already been set. Just off of the dining room in the large family room, the family's Christmas tree still stood even though they'd officially made it to mid-January.

"You still have your Christmas tree up," Dora noted, surprised.

Layla groaned, but Lisa chuckled. "Yes, much to my daughter's horror."

"She keeps it up until, like, Valentine's Day. It's so embarrassing."

"Your mom doesn't keep it up quite that long," Landon contradicted his niece.

"But almost," Logan said, joining the family fray.

"Hey, the way I see it, we should hold on to the Christmas spirit for as long as we can," Lisa said in a way that let Dora know this wasn't the first time she'd uttered that statement.

"It's a gorgeous tree," Dora said, feeling more than a little out of place among the family's easy banter.

She never had this for herself. As a single mom, her mom had had to work multiple jobs to keep a roof over their heads. As a child in her teens, she'd eaten most of her meals in front of the television, alone. From the moment she stepped into the house, she'd been enveloped in a feeling of warmth and family that she had no real reference point for. It was like walking into a Norman Rockwell painting.

Not that she'd never thought about it, having a large loving family. Especially when she and Logan had dated. She'd even begun to let herself hope that one day his family might become hers.

But she needed to remember that was never to be, especially now. Especially after last night. She and Logan were not a couple. They would never be one again. She couldn't let herself get caught up in her feelings for him or fairy-tale dreams.

Heat suddenly flashed through her.

She pushed her chair back away from the table quickly, causing the Elkins' banter to cut off abruptly.

"I think I need a little air."

She darted from the room and to the sliding glass door off of the living room without giving anyone at the table a moment to speak or stop her.

On the back deck, Dora took a deep breath. Someone clearly enjoyed gardening, and it showed in the vibrant colors bursting from the flowerbeds in the backyard.

Behind her, the sliding glass door opened. She was surprised when she glanced over her shoulder and found Lisa stepping out onto the deck instead of Logan.

Lisa handed her a full wineglass. "Are you okay?"

"Yeah." Dora took a big sip of wine. "It was a bit overwhelming, I guess. I'm not used to a large family." *Or any family*, she thought to herself.

"It can be a bit much sometimes, but I wouldn't have it any other way." Lisa smiled. "I'm glad to see you, though. Happy to see you're doing so well."

Dora let her eyes fall to the wood boards of the deck floor. She and Lisa had become something like friends while she and Logan dated. But after the breakup, Dora had stopped taking Lisa's calls. She hadn't wanted to hear the pity in Lisa's voice. Now she wondered if she'd been too quick to toss away the friendship.

"I'm sorry I didn't return your calls after Logan and I..."

Lisa waved away the apology. "You have nothing to apologize for. Breakups are hard. Truth be told, I let Logan know he was an idiot for leaving you, especially in such a cowardly way."

Dora glanced at Lisa, surprised. "You did?"

"Of course." Lisa sighed. "Our family has been through a lot. We're tough, we get through it, but not without scars and making our fair share of mistakes," Lisa said pointedly.

Dora stayed quiet, thinking about her words.

"I'm pretty sure Logan would take back leaving you if he could."

Dora opened her mouth to respond, although she had no idea what she would say.

Lisa held up her hand, warding off Dora's words. "I know I should stay out of it, and I will. But just think about whether you could forgive him. It might be worth it."

Lisa gave her a one-armed hug and headed back into the house as Logan stepped out onto the deck. Lisa winked at him as she passed by and tapped a light punch to Logan's shoulder.

A wink and a punch, Dora thought. Siblings were so confusing.

"Are you okay?" Logan asked.

"Yeah. Just need a little air."

"What were you and my sister talking about so intently out here?"

Dora slid a sidelong glance at him. "You."

"I'm not sure if that's good news or bad news."

Dora chuckled. "Me either."

Logan braced his hand on the deck's railing and leaned closer, desire in his eyes. "Dora, I'm so sorry for leaving."

Dora's heart beat wildly. "Logan..."

He didn't respond. His gaze stayed locked on hers. Her eyes fell to his lips, and she shivered with anticipation. She took a step forward.

The heat from his body enveloped her. He traced her jaw with his thumb.

His lips grace hers, soft, gentle, tentative, as if he couldn't believe she was letting him kiss her. Something familiar stirred inside her, and she leaned in. She kissed him with all the passion and desire that she had been fighting since he walked into the police station's conference room.

He pulled her closer. She shifted, pressing against him and eliciting a groan while his mouth was still pressed against hers.

"Give me a second chance," he said, his arms still around her, his voice low and laced with desire.

"Logan—"

"No, don't answer now. Think about it. I know I messed up. Give me a chance to make it up to you. Give us a chance."

Logan stepped back, though it looked as if it took a fair amount of strength.

Dora watched him disappear, his words playing in her mind. His kiss was still sweet on her lips.

Chapter Eighteen

Despite barely being able to keep her eyes open, Dora slept fitfully. Her dreams were filled with Logan. Somehow, the kiss they'd shared on his sister's deck had gotten to her more than their night of unbridled passion. Sleeping together had brought out something raw and instinctual between them. But the kiss they'd shared... That kiss had burrowed deep inside her and broken feelings open that had been locked up tight for years. Feelings she'd ignored even when they'd been together. The more she relived the kiss, the more right being in Logan's arms—being with him—felt. Although she knew she wasn't ready to tell him that. She wasn't sure when, or if, she ever would be. Opening herself up to him again and trusting him would be one of the hardest things she ever did. She wasn't sure she was brave enough to take the risk, even if she could feel herself falling for him all over again.

Despite the sleepless night, she met Noreen at the gym at 7 am. She hated the gym, but she hadn't found a better way to decompress after a trying day. For her part Noreen loved working out. She said it helped her deal with her aggressions. They ran on side-by-side treadmills, Dora working to keep Logan off her mind by running through the details of the case with Noreen, hoping that her friend and fellow detective might have some advice on how to proceed.

"I'm nearly pulling my hair out," Dora said. "The press, the chief, even Lieutenant Crenshaw...everyone is all over me to find this guy," Dora complained. "He's making the department look like fools."

"High-profile cases are the worst," Noreen agreed.

Dora concurred with Logan's assessment that the killer wouldn't stop until he was caught, but they weren't close to catching him. No matter what they did, he always seemed to stay a few steps ahead of their efforts to capture him. "The fact that the killer appeared to have kidnapped some of his victims in broad daylight is what really has me worried," Dora said. "It means this guy is either extremely confident or insanely reckless. Either way, it makes him very dangerous."

"I wish I had some easy answers for you. I want you to catch this guy as much as everyone else in the department, but you have to just put your head down and keep doing the work."

"You sound like Logan now."

"Oh, I do, do I?" Noreen grinned.

Dora blushed.

"Did something happen between you and the hunky FBI agent?"

Dora stayed silent and ran a little faster.

"It has." Noreen slapped the arm of her machine. "Tell me."

She could resist, but she knew Noreen wouldn't stop her barrage of questions until she got what she wanted.

"We slept together," Dora said, keeping her voice low so no one else would hear.

Too bad Noreen didn't take the hint. Her friend hooted

loudly, drawing the attention of the one other woman in the treadmill section. "I knew it. I knew you two were going to get back together."

"We are not back together," Dora protested, but the words sounded weak to her ear.

"Headed that way."

"We aren't headed anywhere. I think sleeping with him was a mistake. I'm not going to do it again."

Noreen sighed. "Yes, you are."

"What?"

Noreen stopped her machine, and Dora reluctantly followed suit.

"Look, Logan may have moved, but whatever you two had never really ended. It just went dormant for a while. It's obvious you two still have feelings for each other. I know you didn't ask, but I'm taking best-friend privileges and telling you your business anyway. You should see whatever this is with Logan out to the end. Maybe it will be a love affair for the ages. Maybe it peters out once you solve the case, but I think you owe it to yourself to find out. Don't you?"

Dora didn't have time to answer the question before her phone rang.

"Madison," she answered in a tone that was a heavy mix of exhaustion and irritation.

"Dora, we've just gotten a report of another missing woman that fits the profile of our serial killer's victims."

Dora swore, punching the button on the treadmill to stop the machine's belt and hopping off.

"Christine Belgrade," Keene continued. "Reported missing by her boss Tuesday afternoon."

"Yesterday? Why am I just hearing about this now?"

"Damn rookie took the report over the phone but didn't elevate it. The night sergeant caught it and sent it to me."

Later, when she had time, she and that rookie were going to have a serious chat.

Dora glanced at the time on her phone as she headed back to the locker rooms trailed by Noreen who'd received enough sudden phone calls of her own to recognize when duty called. 7:35 a.m. So much for a workout.

She asked Keene to give Logan a call, update him on the situation, and have him pick her up from her house. She pushed her way into the locker room while sending up a quick prayer that they weren't too late to find Christine Belgrade alive and well.

DORA WAS WAITING for him on her front porch when he pulled to a stop in front of her house. He drove them to Wynette Accounting, just blocks from the iconic Union Station where Christine Belgrade worked as a junior accountant. Her boss, Rashida Edwards, had reported her missing. Ms. Edwards had agreed to meet them at her office before it officially opened for business that day. Given the current situation, they were wasting no time in beginning an investigation. Hopefully, Christine was off somewhere taking an impromptu vacation or with a paramour, but she fit the description of their killer's prior victims and Logan had a bad feeling about her disappearance.

He and Dora sat in Rashida Edwards's office.

"Thanks for coming so quickly, Detectives. I'm really worried about Christine," Ms. Edwards said.

"Of course," Dora responded. "When was the last time you saw Christine?"

While Dora did the questioning, Logan took in the woman in front of them. Rashida Edwards was in her mid-forties, slender with the first touches of gray at her temples. Her light brown eyes were shaded and filled with concern behind horn rimmed glasses.

"Yesterday. Christine was only in for a half day. She said she needed the afternoon off."

"Did she say why?"

Rashida shook her head. "No, and I didn't ask. She had the time, so I approved the request. But when she didn't show up for work this morning, I got concerned."

"And you tried to call her?"

"I've called several times, and I went to her house myself. No one answered the phone or the door."

"Could Christine simply have gotten confused? Maybe she thought she'd taken more time off than she actually requested."

"If you knew Christine, you'd know she takes her job very seriously. She's meticulous. You have to be with the job she holds."

"Could there have been some kind of family emergency? Does she have any family that you could check with?"

"She's not married, but she does have a brother. We have an emergency contact for her. I didn't want to worry him unnecessarily." Rashida handed a piece of paper with the name and number on it across her desk to Dora.

Logan understood why the accountant wouldn't want to be the one to make the call letting a brother know his sister might be missing.

"We'll check with her family." Dora slipped the blue sheet of paper between the folds of her notebook and stood. Logan followed. "And I'll need Christine's address."

Ms. Edwards pulled up the map application on her phone and rattled off the address.

"We'll give Christine's house another look and check with her family to see if they have heard from her," Dora said.

Ms. Edwards's brow furrowed. "Please keep me posted. Everyone here loves Chris, and we're all understandably concerned."

She didn't have to add that the serial killer roaming the streets only heightened that concern.

"We'll let you know what we can," Dora promised.

Their next stop was Christine Belgrade's modest, two-bedroom clapboard home just outside of Washington, DC, in the family-friendly suburb of Silver Spring. The driveway was empty, and the house appeared unoccupied from the outside.

On the drive over, Dora placed a call to Christine's emergency contact, her brother, Philip, who lived in Philadelphia. He hadn't heard from Christine in several weeks but claimed that was not unusual for the siblings. He'd been mildly concerned, enough that he told them where to find the spare key to Christine's house and had authorized them to enter to do a wellness check.

Dora headed for the backyard, where she found the hiding rock with the key. "Nothing looks out of place back there," she said, rejoining Logan at the front door.

They made entry, calling out for Christine as they went from room to room through the small house. There was no one there, and it looked as if Christine hadn't slept in her own bed or used the kitchen or bathroom that morning.

"This is not good," Logan stated the obvious.

"No, no, it isn't." Dora pulled her phone from her pocket. "I'm going to put out an APB on Christine's car."

The phone rang in Dora's hand before she made the call.

"Madison," she answered.

Her face blanched and then hardened as she listened to the person on the other end of the line. "We're on our way." She ended the call.

"What is it?" Logan asked, already following her to the door.

"Michelle Quitoni's car was found in Garfield Park. A body was found in the trunk."

Dora drove to Garfield Park in Southeast DC, where Michelle's car had been found. She had a sick feeling in the pit of her stomach that the body that had been found in the car was Christine Belgrade's. But if so, that meant their killer had evolved. Or devolved. That was a question for Logan. Unfortunately, they hadn't said more than to subsist to each other since that morning. How could she have been so stupid? Falling back into bed with him. Clearly, she learned nothing from their disastrous prior relationship and was a glutton for punishment.

I should have moved faster, Dora thought to herself, even though she knew there was nothing she could have done. She pulled up to the curb of the street running alongside the park. She spotted two patrol cars, lights flashing, parked haphazardly. Two male officers were talking to a young woman with hot-pink hair and wearing multicolored leggings. Michelle's car had been found on a service road used by city employees that ran along the southern edge of the park grounds.

Dora and Logan got out of the car and headed toward the officers. She didn't recognize either of them, but one stepped up to her and Logan as they approached. She flashed identification. "Detective Madison. What do we have?"

The twentysomething male officer squinted at her identification before responding, "A female deceased in the trunk. She appears to have been strangled. ME is on his way."

"Do we have a name?" Dora held her breath.

"The car comes back to a Michelle Quitoni." The narrow-eyed look the uniform shot at her let her know he made the obvious connection. "But the identification in the purse in the trunk indicates our body is Christine Belgrade."

"Damn," Logan swore next to Dora.

She shared his frustration but simply pressed her lips together tightly and said a silent prayer for Christine.

Dora nodded at the officer and began walking again along the service road. Logan followed. They hadn't gone far along the road when they spotted the black Audi with silver rims. The trunk was open, and an MPD evidence technician was studiously snapping photos. Curled into a fetal position and wearing a business suit, she was a slender female with dark brown hair. She looked to be in her early thirties. Her eyes were closed and, but for the grayish pallor of her face and her location, it would have been possible to believe she was only sleeping. A red leather purse lay beside her.

A chill ran through Dora as she stared at the woman, who she could not save. She turned toward Logan, who was studying her with concern written all over his face.

"What do you make of the change in MO?"

Logan thought for a moment. "This road is somewhat hidden. My educated guess is he intended to leave the body in the park as he usually does but something happened to interrupt him."

"Something like what?"

"Your guess is as good as mine. Maybe he heard something or got spooked by an animal."

Dora turned to look the way they'd come. "A car could have pulled into the parking lot."

"It's possible," Logan agreed.

"We should check for security video and with patrol units. See if they have reports of anyone being here last night. They might have seen something."

"Okay, so he gets spooked and just leaves Christine here. And why did he still have Michelle's car? I would have thought he'd have dumped it by now."

"All good questions and I'm sorry I can't answer them for you. I can only speculate."

"Speculate away. It's all I got at the moment."

"Well, he could have hung on to the car as a sort of trophy. Or he could have simply not had any idea how to get rid of it without leaving a trail."

"Okay, I'll buy either of those explanations. What concerns me most is how fast he moved on from Michelle to Christine. We only found Michelle's body Monday. There were almost six weeks between our first and second and our second and third victims."

"He's escalating. Possibly devolving. The high he gets from killing is wearing off faster. The media attention may also be affecting him."

"Affecting him how?"

"Contrary to popular belief, not all serial killers relish attention. Or at least not media attention. It makes it harder for them to do what they do. More eyes are looking out for aberrant behaviors. He might feel threatened."

"Great. I take it a serial killer under pressure is—"

"Dangerous. Many can be even more dangerous and unstable than normal, yes."

"Detectives." The officer that had been speaking with the young woman in the leggings when Dora and Logan arrived at the crime scene jogged over to them. "The woman who called the body in would like to be released to go to work."

"I'd like to speak to her first," Dora said. She made her way to where the woman stood chewing on her nail. "Hello. I'm Detective Dora Madison. This is my colleague, Special Agent Elkins. I understand you need to get to work, but I'd like to ask you a few questions."

"I already answered the other agent's questions."

Dora tried to smile, though it was difficult under the circumstances. "I get that. This will be quick, I promise."

The young woman nodded reluctantly.

"Miss..."

"Yvette Jarvis."

"Miss Jarvis, how did you come to be on the service road this morning?"

As unlikely as it was that their killer was a woman, Dora couldn't dismiss any possibility out of hand.

"I always take this route to work. I live in the apartments over there." Yvette waved vaguely to the throng of buildings at her back. The uniform had no doubt gotten the woman's contact information, and Dora would make sure he checked it out. "I work at Nail Serenity, just on the other side of the park. This is the quickest way to work, and I get my steps in."

"Did you see anything or anyone as you walked to work this morning?" Logan stepped in.

"No. No one. Everything was just as it always was until I saw the car. I knew something was up then. Sometimes I see government vehicles on the road. Usually, trucks with garbage or landscaping tools, you know. But never Audis, and mostly on my walk home from work. Almost never in the morning."

"You walk this route home too? Did you come this way yesterday evening?"

Yvette nodded. "Sure did. And before you ask the same question as the other police officer, that car wasn't here."

"What time did you come through here last night?" Dora asked.

Yvette looked up at the sky. "I got off at six, so probably six fifteen, six twenty. Somewhere around there."

She made the call to 911 at 7:50 a.m., so sometime between 6:30ish the night before and 7:50 this morning, their killer had been here. And it was safe to say he'd come after dark, but Dora would put some uniforms on canvassing to see if they could find anyone to definitively narrow down that time frame and, if they were really lucky, give them a description of the perpetrator. She didn't have a lot of faith that they would find working security cameras in the park, not with the city constantly slashing the budget, but she'd get a uniform on finding out for sure. So much work to do. And Dora couldn't help but feel they were miles behind a killer poised to strike again.

Chapter Nineteen

The killer watched gleefully as law enforcement worked around Michelle Quitoni's car. Several of the uniformed officers looked shellshocked, but Detective Dora Madison appeared to be angry. No, not just angry—enraged.

The killer smiled. He'd never been one to hang around and watch the police. It always seemed like a waste of time and an unnecessary risk. He knew the cops kept an eye out for bystanders who appeared a little too interested in their work. It was why he made sure to position himself so he was sure he couldn't be seen from the service road where he'd left Michelle's car.

He watched Detective Madison now. She was with the FBI agent, Elkins. Even though he could tell their conversation was intense, there was also an intimacy about it between them.

Interesting.

So far, following the detective hadn't gotten him much. But he was nothing if not persistent. And it didn't seem like Madison had any idea she was being followed. Some detective. He just needed to be patient. If there was one thing his search for Sarah had taught him, it was patience. It had always paid off for him. He wasn't about to doubt it now.

THE IMAGE OF Christine Belgrade's body folded into the trunk of the Audi gnawed at Dora as Logan drove them to Gabriel Owens's Mount Vernon Square address. Rashida Edwards might not have been aware of Christine's personal relationships, but it was difficult to keep one's personal life completely separate from their professional life. Another coworker had been able to provide Christine's boyfriend's name and address. Keene was back at the station and Dora had him run a quick background check on Gabriel Owens. Other than a charge for misdemeanor drug possession when he was in college, his record was clear. Gabriel was a budding journalist with a handful of bylines to his credit and no steady employment, renting a rundown garden-level apartment.

Logan pulled into the apartment building's parking lot next to a beige Cadillac, and together they headed up the walkway to Gabriel's apartment. It was never easy to deliver the news that a loved one had died. Even worse when a loved one had been taken violently.

"I hate death notifications," Dora said.

"Me too," Logan concurred. "It's the worst part of the job."

Dora rang the bell. A moment later, the apartment door opened. Standing there was a tall and muscular man in his mid-twenties with dark disheveled hair and a thick beard. "Yes?"

Dora and Logan introduced themselves and flashed their credentials. "Mr. Owens?"

The man in front of them hesitated. "Yes. Do you want to tell me what this is about?"

"Can we come inside? Please?" Dora added when the man in front of them still hesitated.

"It's about Christine Belgrade," Logan added.

"Yeah, come in." He held the door open for them to pass through.

They stepped through the door, and Dora glanced around the small, slightly musty-smelling apartment. The furnishings were sparse. A well-loved sofa sat across from a flat-screen and a card table served as a dinner table. Very *bachelor lives here*. A Jack Russell terrier lay beside the sofa. He lifted his head when Logan and Dora entered but apparently found them uninteresting and lowered it a moment later.

"What's her name?" Logan nodded at the dog.

Gabriel glanced over at the sofa. "Jack. Not very original, I know. I'm sorry—I'm a little frazzled. Would either of you like something to drink?"

"No, that's okay," Dora said. "Can we sit?" Dora gestured to the sofa.

Gabriel led them to the sofa. "What is this about Chris? Is she okay?"

"Unfortunately, she isn't." Dora had learned long ago that it was best to rip the Band-Aid off when delivering bad news. "I regret to inform you she has been killed."

Gabriel blinked rapidly. "Dead? How?"

"We're still very early in our investigation, but it looks like she was murdered. I'm sorry," Dora said again.

Gabriel's shoulders slumped, and an expletive slipped from his lips.

Dora gave him a moment to process the news before asking, "When did you last see Christine?"

Gabriel ran a hand across his beard. "A few days ago. Saturday. We went to the farmer's market. And we spoke Monday morning."

"Weren't you concerned about not having heard from her?"

"Not at all," Gabriel replied. "We don't speak every day. In fact, we can go for several days without speaking. We had agreed to keep our relationship casual for now."

Dora regarded the man in front of her skeptically. "Do you mind telling us where you were last night?"

"I was out with some friends at Carmella's, a bar on U Street. We had drinks, then went to dinner. We met there at around seven and were together until around eleven. I know I got home just before midnight."

Dora got the names and contact numbers for Gabriel's friends. She'd have his alibi checked out, but her gut told her that Gabriel Owens wasn't their guy. He seemed genuinely upset about Christine's death.

"Christine's boss told us that Christine took Monday afternoon off from work. Do you have any idea where she was going?"

Gabriel rubbed his beard again. "I'm not exactly sure. I know she said she had a doctor's appointment, though."

Gabriel wasn't able to tell them the name of the doctor, but it was something to look into.

He was unable to provide them any more information that they found helpful.

Dora's phone rang as they left Gabriel's apartment. The conversation was brief.

"That didn't sound good," Logan said when she ended the call.

"It wasn't. Lieutenant Crenshaw wants to see us. Now."

LATE THAT AFTERNOON, the task force met again. Dora stood in front of the assembled group: Lieutenant Crenshaw, Roberts, Keene and Logan. She briefed on what little information they had at the point and Christine Belgrade's murder. She and Logan had already met with Lieutenant Crenshaw privately, where the lieutenant had recounted the not-so-pleasant call she'd received from the chief on behalf of Senator Quitoni. Not surprisingly, the senator and his wife were furious that Dora hadn't arrested their daughter's killer yet. They wanted her taken off the case. Dora had held her breath, waiting for Crenshaw's dismissal to slam into her. Surprisingly, the chief hadn't given in, standing behind his lieutenant and the department. But Crenshaw had warned that support was soft and could disappear at any moment. As if Dora wasn't under enough pressure. All she could do was do her job, so she got to it. She turned her attention to the monitor on the wall of the conference room.

She brought up images of the third and fourth victims, Michelle and Christine. "Christine Belgrade was murdered sometime between Monday afternoon when she left work early and this morning when her body was found in the trunk of Michelle Quitoni's car. The medical examiner is working on the autopsy, but there was writing on Christine's legs—the same phrase found on the other three bodies. A desert rose was found in the front passenger seat of the car. We believe the killer was spooked prior to setting out the body as he usually does. Evidence techs are gathering evidence at the scene and towing the car to their facility for further processing. So far, there is no known connection between Christine and any of our prior victims."

She went over all the victims' vital information again, the location of the murders, and the efforts thus far to gather evidence and interview witnesses, including the improbability of John Leonard being their killer. She did not try to hide her own frustration with the pace of the investigation and the lack of a viable suspect.

Dora swallowed as she looked at Logan.

He gave her a nod and stood, taking her place at the

front of the room. "Losing another woman was something none of us wanted to happen. But this recent murder tells us a lot about our killer." He reiterated the points he made to Dora earlier about the murderer possibly evolving in his methods. "One thing I am sure of is that this killer has no intention of stopping—not until we stop him."

Dora stepped up next to Logan, and they fielded questions from the room. Most of which came from Lieutenant Crenshaw, and many of which they had no answers for yet. The meeting began to wind down as Keene's phone beeped.

The frown that bloomed on Keene's face was enough to have Dora moving across the room to his side before he finished reading the text message.

"What is it?" she asked him, something more than seeing Logan reach her side.

Keene looked up from his phone. "It's the media. They've gotten Randi Singer's name."

DORA HAD LOGAN drive her to Violet Fullerton's house after the task-force meeting broke up. Randi was understandably upset and scared. It had taken an hour to calm her down and convince her that she was still safer at Violet's house than out on the street by herself. She finally agreed to remain at Violet's house, but Dora wasn't sure how much longer Randi would be willing to be "held prisoner," as she'd described it. But for now, she was safe. The press might have had her name, but they didn't know where she was, and they wouldn't if Dora had anything to say about it.

It was after eight when Logan finally pulled the car into her driveway. Without asking he walked her to her door following her inside. She didn't have the energy or desire to stop him.

She headed back to the kitchen.

"You've been quiet all day," Logan said, taking off his suit jacket and tossing it over a chair at the kitchen table.

"Just thinking about everything." She reached into the fridge and grabbed a bottle of water. "This case is…"

"A tough one. For everyone. But I don't think that's all this is. You've been avoiding me."

She closed the fridge door with more force than she'd intended. "What are you talking about? We've been working together all day."

"Yes, and you've barely looked at me and only spoken to me when you absolutely had to."

"That's not avoiding you."

Logan shook his head, a rueful smile on his face. "It's not going to work, you know."

"What's not going to work?" Dora crossed her arms over her chest.

"Ignoring me. Pushing me away."

"I'm not doing any of that. I just need to solve this case. This maniac is killing women in my city."

"You are one of the best cops I know. One of the best detectives in this city. But this is not about the case. This is about us."

"There is no *us*."

He took a step closer to her. "You may want that to be the case, but I think we both know it isn't. Not only is there an *us*, I think there is always going to be an *us*. We've gotten under each other's skin in a way that doesn't dim. It doesn't falter. It doesn't go away. It just is. We can try to ignore it, but I don't want to, and I don't think you do either."

She huffed a laugh. "You're pretty full of yourself."

His smile turned seductive, and despite everything she'd just said to him, her body reacted.

"I care about you, Dora."

His words sent emotions swirling inside of her including fear. Because he wanted her to admit that she cared about him too. Which she did, but she didn't know if she could get over the fear that he'd leave again, and she didn't know if she could stand losing him a second time.

"You left. And I didn't hear from you for two years."

Logan took another step closer to her. They were only inches apart now. "The biggest mistake of my life. If I could do it over again I would. But I can only promise you that if you give us a second chance, I will never hurt you again."

She rested her forehead against his. "I'm afraid."

He huffed a laugh. "Me too." He brushed a strand of hair back from her face. "So, let's be afraid together."

He didn't move, and she knew he was waiting for her. He was waiting for her to decide if they would move forward together or go on with their lives separately but always wondering what might have been. What if she'd opened up her heart again? What if she'd forgiven him? Yes, he had hurt her when he'd left, but he was there now. They had this second chance. If she didn't take it, she'd be the one hurting them both. Because she was sure he was right. They had gotten under each other's skins in a way that was irreversible. He was her person. The one she was supposed to walk through this life with. She just had to reach out and grab him.

She lifted her gaze, a single tear sliding down her cheek as she pressed her lips to his.

He stood frozen for a moment more before, wrapping his arms around her and pulling her tightly against his chest.

She could feel how much he wanted her, his desire matched only by her own.

Dora took his hand and led him to the bedroom. Moments later they were on the bed, stripping each other of their clothing. Then they were tangled together, Logan's weight pressing her down into the mattress.

Dora wrapped her legs around Logan's waist and took him into her body in one smooth movement. He filled her, and they moved together, their desire building in waves until it reached an explosive crescendo.

Then they were over the peak and free-falling, holding on to each other more tightly than she'd ever held on to anything before.

Chapter Twenty

When she woke the next morning, contentment had given way to concern. She'd promised herself that this would be nothing more than a casual fling. Once they caught their killer, she'd go back to her life, and he'd go back to his. But that was a lie—maybe it had always been. Because what she was feeling wasn't casual. It was so much more than that. So much more intense and...real. And once again she feared her heart was on the line, ready to be crushed a second time.

Her phone rang, and as she sat up to get it, Logan reached out for her, attempting to tug her back down on the bed. She evaded his grasp. The phone was still in her jacket pocket, which lay tossed haphazardly on the floor next to the bed. Aware that she was naked, she slipped the jacket on before she pulled her phone out of the pocket and accepted the call.

Keene was on the other end of the line. He started speaking without preamble. "The evidence technicians found something in Michelle Quitoni's car."

"Do you want to tell me what it is?" Dora said.

"Let me have my moment." Another short pause. "It's a pill bottle."

"There better be more," Dora growled.

"Patience. Patience. The bottle was wedged under the driver seat, which is why we didn't see it at the scene. It's the name on the bottle though that's important," Keene said, on a roll now. "It's not Michelle's. It's Waylen Osvolo's."

Dora's heartbeat quickened with excitement she recognized as born from having finally caught a break. "Now, why would Osvolo's prescription bottle be in Michelle's car?" She felt the bed move as Logan stood up. She felt rather than saw that he was also now fully engaged in her and the phone call.

"Well, that's something I'm sure you want to find out." Dora could hear the smile in Keene's voice.

"You're right about that."

"You want me to call Elkins for you?"

Dora glanced over her shoulder again. Logan was shrugging into his shirt, having already pulled on his pants. She took a moment to admire his sculpted abs before the fabric hid them from her view. "No, I'll call in. I still don't have a car, so I'll need him to pick me up anyway. We'll go pick up Osvolo and bring him in." She ended the call with Keene, then relayed what he had said to Logan, though he had picked up on most of it already.

She glanced at the bedside clock. It was after eight in the morning, and they still needed to shower before they could go get their suspect.

"We should shower, then try to find Osvolo at his job."

Logan circled the bed to come stand in front of her. "I like the sound of a shower, especially if you share it with me."

Dora's eyes shifted away from his. "I don't know if that's a good idea. We need to focus on this case."

Logan reached out and cupped her cheek. "I know I

messed up last time, but I'm not going to make the same mistake twice. I think we have something here. And I think you know that. Whatever you have to do to prove to you that I'm not the same guy that ran away from you... I'll do it."

She wanted to believe him. Even if it didn't work out, she didn't want to give up whatever time she had with Logan now.

Dora stepped around him and headed for the en suite bathroom. At the door she turned, unsurprised to find Logan watching her. She let the jacket fall off her shoulders and onto the floor. She arched her back. "I thought you wanted to shower. What are you waiting for?"

THE SHOWER WAS quick but very satisfying. Logan had trouble forcing himself to focus on the task at hand even as he pulled the car to the gates of the Sutton Place community. This time the gatehouse was manned by a rent-a-cop who directed them to the management offices.

A woman in her early sixties with a platinum-blond bob and too much makeup met them in the management office. She introduced herself as Geraldine Steward.

"Mr. Osvolo has been let go."

"Let go?" Dora said incredulously.

Logan shared her incredulity. They finally had a good lead, and now they didn't know where to find him.

"Yes, as of two days ago."

"May I ask why?" Dora bit out.

"Well, we don't usually discuss personnel matters, but as you are the police... We discovered Mr. Osvolo stealing from one of the residents."

"Stealing? Stealing what? There was no report made to the police department." She knew that if there had been,

Osvolo's name would have triggered an alert to her since he was a person of interest in a murder investigation.

"No, the board thought it best not to report it, and the homeowner agreed. The community doesn't need any more bad press."

Bad press, Logan assumed, was referring to Michelle Quitoni, as if the most important thing regarding the murder of one of her neighbors was the inconvenience to her. He felt his mouth turn down in a frown. "What did Mr. Osvolo steal?" he asked instead of saying what he wanted to say to the woman.

"Clothing."

"He broke into someone's house?"

"Not exactly," the woman said.

"Mrs. Steward, I'm sure it will be more than just bad press for your neighborhood if I have to arrest you for impeding a criminal investigation," Dora said.

"You wouldn't dare." The older woman glared at Dora.

"Try me," Dora spat back. "Now, what is this about Osvolo stealing clothes?"

Mrs. Steward huffed. "A resident put a bag of clothes out on her stoop to be picked up by a charity. She went out to run some errands, and when she returned Mr. Osvolo was on her property going through the bags. It was clear he was taking out things he intended to keep for himself. She reported the attempted theft, and of course, the board agreed we had to act swiftly. We can't have anyone untrustworthy working for us."

"Do you have any idea where Mr. Osvolo is now?"

Mrs. Steward shook her head. "None."

Dora and Logan left the office and stepped back into the warm morning sunlight. Dora slipped her sunglasses on. "They never make it easy, do they?"

"I'm Detective Dora Madison." Dora held her badge out for Waylen's wife, Cindy, to peer at it through the screen door. The address on Waylen Osvolo's driver's license belonged to a small clapboard house in the family-friendly neighborhood of Woodridge.

"Are you Mrs. Cindy Osvolo?"

"Yes."

"We need to speak to your husband. Is he here?"

"He doesn't live here anymore. He hasn't lived here for almost four months now."

Logan could feel his frustration growing.

"Do you mind if we come in and take a look around?" Dora asked.

Cindy hesitated for a moment before pushing the screen door open and standing aside. The house was lived in, with shoes lined up at the door and mismatched furniture in the living room. Dora could see into the eat-in kitchen with its yellow appliances and scarred linoleum floors.

But Osvolo was not inside.

Logan and Dora made their way back to the living room where Cindy waited. "I told you he wasn't here."

"Do you have any idea where he might be?"

Cindy shook her head. "Waylen hasn't been around for months. Not since I kicked him out for cheating on me. The best I can tell you is that he always has liked Miller's Bar over on U Street. You might find him there."

Dora made a note of it in her notebook.

"Mrs. Osvolo—"

"I'm changing my name back to *Fairmont* just as soon as the divorce is final."

"Ms. Fairmont," Logan started again, "have you ever heard the names *Christine Belgrade* or *Michelle Quitoni*?"

Cindy's face scrunched in thought. "No, I don't think so."

Logan tossed out the two other victims' names, but Cindy didn't recognize them either. There was nothing else to get from Osvolo's estranged wife, so he thanked Cindy for her time and left.

The door closed behind them before they made it off the front stoop.

"I take it Miller's Bar is our next stop," Logan said as they made their way to the car.

Dora nodded. "Third time. It's got to be the charm, right?"

Logan hoped she was right.

MILLER'S BAR OPENED at five in the afternoon, but a brief chat with the owner and weekday bartender revealed that most of the regulars like Osvolo didn't put in an appearance before eight in the evening. Dora stationed a couple of rookie detectives in plain clothes in the bar right after opening just in case Osvolo made an early appearance. She and Logan arrived just before eight and ordered drinks taking them to a booth in the back corner. The two detectives she had on duty were relieved by two fresh pairs of eyes, and then they waited.

Dora scanned the growing group of patrons with sharp eyes. She started when Logan reached across the table and took her hand in his.

"You need to relax. Osvolo isn't here yet, but if he's our killer, he might make a run for it he spots us."

Dora took a deep breath and let it out, sliding her hand from under Logan's. He was right about relaxing, but there was no way she could do that with her hand in his.

"We need to be ready. We have to assume that he's armed and dangerous."

"True, which is why we can't scare him off. We need to take him down as quickly and quietly as possible."

"Maybe we should have tried to catch him as he came in," she said. "He'd have been easier to spot." Dora second-guessed herself.

They spent the hours between talking to Osvolo's wife and getting to the bar, running through the best scenarios for the takedown. Miller's was a popular place on a street full of popular establishments. Even on a weekday evening the pedestrian traffic was fixed. The team had ultimately agreed it would be safest to corner Osvolo inside the bar rather than outside.

"There's no looking back now," Logan said. "We just need to do what we do best."

"Agreed," Dora said.

"Good. Just make sure you stay close to me," he added. "Everyone goes home in one piece tonight."

Holding his gaze, she understood that he was probably thinking about their last outing to bring in a suspect and their subsequent car crash. She knew he wanted to protect her, and she felt the same way about him, but this was the job. For both of them.

Dora's eyes roamed over the crowd, on the lookout again for Osvolo. Maybe he wasn't coming tonight. He had just lost his job. Maybe he'd decided to tighten his belt, lay off the boozing and bars until he found a new one.

Or maybe not. Dora homed in on the man who had just come through the doors and was sidling up to the bar.

"That's him," she said, already sliding out of the booth.

Logan followed. "Hopefully, Osvolo will come quietly."

Osvolo spotted them then. He jumped up from the bar stool he'd been sitting on, pushing through a group of women who'd approached the bar, and ran.

"Spoke too soon," Logan deadpanned.

Dora took off after Osvolo with Logan hot on her heels. They dodged bar goers as they tried to reach Osvolo before he made it back onto the street. It was slow going as many of the patrons were clueless to what was going on. And it didn't appear that the other two detectives she had in the bar were having any easier time reaching their suspect.

Just when Osvolo made it to the front entrance of the bar, a burly security guard stepped in his path. Osvolo bounced off the man comically. The barman reached out to steady him but held on to him while Osvolo struggled.

Nora reached the bear, taking Osvolo from the bouncer and twisting his arms behind his back, cutting him.

"Waylen Osvolo, you are being arrested on suspicion of murder."

Osvolo's attitude hadn't improved at the police station. He was still defiant, proclaiming that he'd had nothing to do with Michelle's murder and that he was going to sue the department, the FBI, and a host of other people. He was speaking to them, though, so Dora was willing to put up with his puffery.

Logan and Dora sat on one side of the table in the interrogation room. Osvolo was seated on the opposite side of the table with a dour expression on his face. He looked as if he had a rough go of it, which, Logan realized, was true. Osvolo sported a scruffy beard and bloodshot eyes. He looked as if he hadn't slept in days.

Logan had noted a small cut on the back of Osvolo's right hand when he cuffed him to the table and pointed it out to Dora. Could it have possibly happened when he killed Christine? Maybe they get lucky and there would be DNA this time.

Osvolo had declined to have a lawyer present, so Dora got right to the questioning. "Mr. Osvolo, you are being held on suspicion of having a hand in the murder of Michelle Quitoni."

Osvolo's nostrils flared. "I had nothing to do with any murders. I didn't kill anybody."

"Where were you from Monday at noon until Tuesday at eight in the morning?" Dora's tone gave nothing away, but she narrowed her eyes at Osvolo, studying him.

He provided an answer that amounted to "Alone at home," so he had no real alibi.

"Where is home these days, Mr. Osvolo?" Logan said. "We understand from your wife that you no longer reside with her."

"I've been bunking on a buddy's sofa ever since that witch put me out of my own house."

Dora and Logan had been switching off on the questioning in an attempt to keep Osvolo off-kilter.

Logan tsked. "Things haven't been going so well for you lately, Waylen. We understand you've lost your job," Logan said.

"What about it?" Osvolo shot back

"Well, Geraldine Steward said you were caught stealing. Is that true?"

"It wasn't stealing. How can you steal something from someone giving the thing away?"

"Fair point," Dora said, taking the good cop role for a moment. "Let's call it 'taking,' then. Have you ever taken anything else that belongs to a resident in the neighborhood where you previously worked?"

"I don't know what you mean."

"Say a car, perhaps," Logan jumped in again.

"Now you're accusing me of being a car thief. I guess it's better than a murderer." Osvolo scowled.

"It doesn't have to be one or the other. You could have murdered Michelle Quitoni, then kept her car to make it easier to grab and transport your next victim," Dora responded.

"I told you I didn't murder anyone."

"Then how did this—" Dora slapped a photo of the pill bottle down on the table "—pill bottle, get into Michelle Quitoni's car?"

Osvolo visibly swallowed. "I don't know anything about that. I don't even know what it is." But beads of sweat had broken out on his forehead.

"You don't know, huh?" Logan picked up the questioning. "Let me help you, then. It's a prescription bottle of Oxy with your name on it, and I bet you can guess where we found it."

"Why should I… How could I know?"

"We found it in Michelle Quitoni's car. Where we also found the body of Christine Belgrade."

"I don't know anyone named Christine Belgrade," Osvolo yelled. "And I didn't kill anyone. Stop saying that I did."

"How did the pill bottle get into Michelle's car?" Logan pressed.

Osvolo was close to cracking. "I don't know… I don't know."

Dora slammed her palm against the metal table. "Don't give us that. We got a pill bottle with your name on it in a dead woman's car with another dead woman in the trunk. You are in this up to your eyeballs. If you aren't a serial killer, I'd bet dollars to doughnuts you know who is."

"Look, I don't know anything about murder. I admit I

sold the Oxy to Michelle. She came asking if I knew anyone who could sell her something more recreational than weed. I've been prescribed Oxy for a back injury—I got in a car accident last year. I didn't like how the pills made me feel, but a buddy of mine bought them off me for a decent chunk of change. I found a doctor that didn't ask too many questions, and I kept buying them for my buddy, so when Michelle asked, I offered. That's all I know."

"So, you lied about how close you and Michelle were earlier. You aren't just the property manager. You were her dealer," Dora said.

"I'm not a drug dealer or a killer."

Logan cocked his head to the side, studying their prime suspect. There was a lot to suggest they had their guy, but something wasn't sitting right with him. "What about a voyeur? Are you still a Peeping Tom, Waylen?"

They found the juvenile record right before coming into the interrogation room. It wouldn't be admissible in court, but that didn't mean they couldn't use it to break Osvolo. Whatever it took, if he was their serial killer. Osvolo stilled, his face going blank. It was as if he'd gone somewhere else.

"Mr. Osvolo, could you answer the question?" Logan pressed.

Osvolo snapped back to attention. "No, no, I don't think I will. In fact, I want my lawyer. Now."

They had no choice but to end the interview.

Lieutenant Crenshaw met them in the hallway. "We can hold him on charges stemming from selling the Oxy, but we don't have enough to arrest him for the murders."

"We'll get enough," Dora declared. "This is our guy. I can feel it."

"I'm not so sure," Logan replied hesitantly. He didn't

want to undermine Dora in front of her superior, but there were quite a few holes in the tale of Osvolo as a serial killer.

"What do you mean?" Dora argued.

"It's just I don't think we should get out ahead of our skis here. The lieutenant is right about the evidence being insufficient for charges, and Osvolo doesn't fit the profile of our serial killer."

"What are you talking about? White male between the ages of twenty-nine and forty-five. He's even got a peeping charge, and who knows what else we'll find?"

"Superficially, yes, he could be our guy, but we have no connection between him and the other victims. And usually, serial killers have some kind of trauma that leads them down the road of killing. We found nothing like that in Osvolo's past."

"We will," Dora gritted out.

"Fine." Crenshaw put her hands up, signaling to cease the bickering. "Well, find the evidence, then. If Osvolo is our guy, I want to nail him to the wall."

Chapter Twenty-One

The killer had been right about following the detective paying off. Detective Madison had led him right to her witness, thanks to some help from the press. It was about time they did something besides turn up the heat on him.

He'd been by the house where Detective Madison's witness was staying several times in the last twenty-four hours. He had to be careful. Despite what some law enforcement thought about serial killers, generally he had no desire to get caught. But now it was time to put his plan into motion.

The killer made his way around the side of the small home he had followed Detective Madison to the day before. The interior was dark. He watched a middle-aged woman and a second young woman in her late teens leave minutes earlier. He couldn't imagine what a middle-aged woman would have been doing in the park in the middle of the night, which meant the witness was probably the younger woman. Not that it mattered. He'd take care of both of them. No loose ends.

He made his way to the back door of the house. It was easy to force the door open with a heavy rock he took from the garden. Inside, he found a small functional space. He didn't need to turn on any lights, and he was careful not to touch anything. As long as the occupants of the home came in through the front door, they wouldn't realize anyone was here until it was too late. He planned to take care of the middle-aged woman first, but as soon as he saw the younger one, he'd known that it was no coincidence that she was the one who'd spotted him the night he left Michelle. It had been fate.

She looked just like his Sarah.

He passed the kitchen and the living room and climbed the stairs to the second floor of the home. There were three bedrooms, although one was more the size of a closet. Someone had turned that room into an office. The largest bedroom was easily identifiable as the older woman's. The bed was made and covered with a crocheted blanket. The dresses in the closet were sensible and hung above equally sensible shoes.

The last bedroom was a woman's as well but clearly a younger woman's space. A pair of jeans lay thrown across the bottom of an unmade bed, and the dresser drawer hung partially open. There was a small armoire, but it was empty inside. A notebook sat on an otherwise empty desk.

He fingered through it quickly, becoming bored with the overwrought complaints that the younger woman seemed to have with the old one. There'd be no need for his Sarah to worry after tonight. Not after he got her home. Then she would have everything she needed, and she'd be happy.

So would he.

The killer smiled.

It wouldn't be long now.

DORA WORKED WELL into the evening, digging through Osvolo's recent and distant past, looking for some connection to any of the victims other than Michelle and a trigger for his homicidal tendencies. She found nothing. Osvolo might have been a threat, but there was nothing in his past that she could find to prove he was a murderer. She was frustrated. Even more so because she was beginning to wonder if Logan was right and Osvolo wasn't their guy, after all.

At nine that night, Logan shut down his laptop and stood. "We should go home."

"You go. There is still some stuff I want to get done here."

"Dora, I had to give my professional opinion. It's what your department is paying me the big bucks for."

"Of course you did."

Logan sighed heavily. "You're going to burn out if you don't get some rest."

"I'll rest when we know our serial killer is behind bars."

"Let me take you home."

"The requisitions department issued me a shiny new police sedan." A clerk had dropped off the keys when Logan had stepped out to get dinner, an invitation that Dora had declined. "I can get myself home now. But thanks for all the rides."

Logan sighed again. "Then let me come home with you."

Dora glanced around the bullpen. Most of the detectives had gone home hours ago, but the skeleton night crew was there. No one seemed to be paying her or Logan any attention, though.

"I don't think that's a good idea," she said, keeping her voice low. Then, before he could speak again: "I need time and space to think. I can't do that with you around. Anyway, you probably want to stop by Landon's place on your way home anyway."

Logan cocked his head to the side, confused.

"Look in your bag. I think you have something for him," Dora said, before turning back to her computer monitor.

Logan reached into his bag and found a single manila folder that hadn't been there before. He fingered through the first pages, recognizing them as the twenty-year-old report on his father's murder investigation.

"Thank you," he said softly.

Dora waved him off.

Logan studied her for a long moment before speaking. "Good night, Dora."

She met his gaze and gave him a small smile. "Good night, Logan."

DORA WALKED THROUGH the police garage, headed for her newly minted police-issued sedan, when her cell rang. "This is Madison."

"Detective Madison, you have to help me." The breathy words came over the line in a whisper.

"Randi? What's going on? What's wrong?"

"There is someone here. Someone in Violet's house. I think Violet is hurt badly."

Dora ran the rest of the way to the car and jumped in. "Where are you right now?"

"I'm hiding in a closet, but I can hear the guy. He's still here."

Dora tore out of the garage. "Can you get out of the house?"

"I can't." Dora could hear the tears in Randi's voice. "I'm scared."

"Randi, I'm on my way. I'm minutes away. Just be quiet. I'm going to switch over to the other line now and make a call. Don't hang up. I'll be right back, okay?"

"Okay."

Dora put Randi's call on hold and used the police radio to call for backup to Violet's house. Then she punched in Logan's number. Logan's phone rang but rolled over to voicemail.

She made the turn off the main road and into Violet's neighborhood. "Logan, it's Dora. Randi is in trouble. Someone broke into Violet's house. I'm almost there. I've called for backup, but...call me."

She flipped back to Randi's call as she turned onto Violet's street.

"Randi?" Dora said but received no answer. Her heart hammered. She didn't want to yell just in case her voice carried over the phone in case the perpetrator was still there, and the sound clued him into Randi's hiding place.

She tried again. "Randi?"

Still no answer.

Dora threw the car into Park in front of the house next door to Violet's. There was no time to wait for backup.

The street appeared quiet. Violet's house was dark. She peered through the sidelights next to the front door. The inside of the house was still. The door was locked. She made her way around the back, her gaze catching on the busted lock on the back door. Her pulse raced, adrenaline soaring through her body.

She stepped into the small vestibule between the kitchen and the laundry room and listened. The refrigerator hummed. A pipe clanked somewhere in the walls. She could hear a rhythmic ticking that she recognized as being the pendulum on a grandfather clock coming from the front of the house.

She moved as quickly and quietly as she could along the main floor. The house wasn't large. The kitchen, living room, dining room, and a small den comprised the main floor.

Dora climbed the stairs to the second floor. Randi had said she was hiding in the closet, which could've been any closet, but at this time of night the bedroom closet seemed as likely as any.

The quiet stillness of the house was disconcerting. The first, largest bedroom looked disheveled, as if a struggle had occurred, but there was no one in the room. Dora stepped back into the hallway, her senses picking up the whisper of a sound a split second too late.

She turned, but not fast enough. A burst of pain blinded her.

Then there was darkness.

LOGAN SAT AT Landon's kitchen table, nursing a beer. Landon sat across from him, flipping through the Metropolitan Police file on their father's case. His brother had given him a summary of all the research he'd done over the last several days and his visit with Carisse Lynn's sandwich shop. Logan still wasn't sure whether his brother was on to something or on a wild-goose chase, but he knew that Landon needed to assure himself that everything that could be done to catch their father's killer had been done. But it seemed farfetched to believe that their father's death might have had something to do with Addison Kober's disappearance. It was far more likely, in Logan's opinion, that Landon was grasping at straws.

"You have to thank Dora for me."

"You may want to thank her yourself." Logan took another pull from his beer bottle.

Landon looked up from the file. "Things are going that well?"

Logan sighed. "I'm not sure how things are going."

"It looked like you two were getting along at family dinner the other night at Lisa's."

Logan ran his finger through the condensation on the beer bottle. "I told her how I feel about her."

Landon's left eyebrow arched. "And how do you feel about her?"

"I love her. I've loved her for a long time." It felt good to say that. "I was an idiot to leave her."

"Well, it seems like you're making a good start at fixing things."

"I thought so." Logan frowned.

"Dora wasn't receptive?"

"Well, I invited her to come home with me tonight, and she said she needed time to think."

"Ouch."

"Imagine how I feel."

"Well, she didn't say get lost, so there's still a chance."

"Just what every man wants to hear after he bares his soul to the woman he loves—*there's still a chance*." He finished his beer.

Landon stood. "Let me get you another beer."

Logan's phone vibrated. He took it from his pocket and saw that he had a message from Dora. The phone hadn't rung, but their mother's house had always been iffy when it came to cellular service.

Logan accessed his voicemail and listened to the message. He was out of his chair and headed to the front door before the message was over.

"Logan, where are you going?" Landon said, racing behind him to the door.

"It's Dora," Logan called back over his shoulder without stopping. "She's headed into trouble."

Dora was missing, likely in the hands of the serial killer, and Logan had no idea where to begin looking for her. A neighbor had given them a description of a vehicle that had been seen speeding away from the house: a white SUV with a black racing stripe. It matched the description of the vehicle registered to Violet Fullerton. They already had an APB out on it. Violet had been in critical condition when Logan arrived. She was barely breathing but hanging on. An ambulance had raced her to the hospital. Now the evidence-collection team was in the house and Logan had been relegated to the front yard to question witnesses and wait.

Keene joined Logan in the driveway.

"I got our tech department looking at traffic cams to see if we can get a sense of which direction the perp is going," Keene continued.

Logan took out his cell phone and texted Kaj's information to Keene. "Tell them to reach out to Kaj Ryland. He's a computer expert at the FBI. If there's something to be found on those traffic cams, he'll find it."

"Will do."

Logan's phone rang. Crenshaw's number scrolled across the screen. He answered with "Tell me you have something."

"Traffic cams caught a white SUV heading across the Washington, DC–Maryland border about forty-five minutes ago. We've got state units on the lookout for it."

Logan brought up a map on his phone, looking for any ideas as to where their perp might be headed. But without knowing who they were looking for it was impossible to say.

"Elkins. Keene." Roberts jogged toward them. "We've got him. We got a face on a neighbor's doorbell camera."

"Crenshaw, I have to call you back," Logan said.

"Keep me posted, and send me that video, Roberts," Crenshaw said before ending the call.

Roberts pressed Play on the video already cued up on his phone. After a few seconds of nothing but the street in front of a nearby house, a man walked into the frame from the left. His head was down so his face couldn't be seen.

"Roberts, this doesn't show us anything we can use."

"Wait for it." Roberts fast-forwarded. "Watch when the car backs out of the driveway and turns. Here." Roberts paused the video and enlarged the screen, turning it to face outward so they could all see it.

Logan's stomach dropped.

"It's a money shot," Keene said.

"I can get it out on the wires right away," Roberts said. "Someone will definitely recognize this guy."

"You don't have to put it out," Logan said. "I know who it is."

Chapter Twenty-Two

Pain thundered through Dora's head, so loud it was all she could hear. It pounded against her brain like a hammer. Her thoughts came slowly, as if she was swimming against a powerful tide of pain and fear. *Where am I?* In a car, she realized as the ground rolled underneath her.

Panic raced through her. She opened her eyes to darkness. A blindfold covered her face. That realization brought another stab of fear.

Don't panic. And don't let on that you are awake.

She wasn't sure why, but she instinctively knew that letting her captor know she was conscious would not be good if she had any chance of getting out of this alive. She didn't want to draw any attention. She didn't have her gun, so surprise was her best asset at the moment. Her hands were tied behind her back, but the car's carpeting against her face was rough enough that it did not take much to shift the blindfold covering her eyes so that she could see. She and Randi lay in the trunk of what appeared to be an SUV. Randi was unconscious, but the slight rise and fall of her chest let Dora know she was still alive. For now. Matted blood covered her left temple, and there was little color in her face. Dora had to get Randi to help soon, or escaping would be the least of their problems.

A cold sweat seeped from her pores as she tried to think of what to do. Where was their captor taking them? The headache pulsing in her head made it hard to think, much less come up with a coherent plan.

The car rolled on for how long, Dora wasn't sure. The drive had gone from smooth to bumpy at some point, telling her that they'd turned off the paved streets and onto what was probably an unpaved road somewhere. Somewhere no one would ever find them, the thought ran through her head.

No. She couldn't think that way. She had to come up with a plan. She glanced at Randi again. She was still out cold; her breathing had become raspy. If Dora didn't come up with a plan, she and Randi would just be two more missing women among thousands, dumped in some remote outpost somewhere where no one would ever find them. She'd never get the chance to tell Logan how she really felt. That she forgave him. That she wanted to have a life with him. That she loved him and had loved him almost since the moment they'd met. She would have that chance. She just had to not panic and think.

She took as deep a breath as she could without making any sound.

Her head bounced against the floor as the car drove over a deep pothole before jerking to a stop.

Her pulse raced. She held her breath as the SUV's front door opened, then slammed shut. She wheeled herself to say still, to keep her breathing even, but nothing could stop the frantic pounding of her heart.

The trunk opened, and she was grabbed by the ankles and dragged out of the car, her body dumped against the gravel strewn ground.

A dark silhouette loomed over her. A low voice sounded near her ear. "I know you're conscious, Detective."

Dora went rigid. She recognized that voice.

She squinted up at her captor and found herself staring at Dr. Najimy.

L̲ogan felt like he was going to jump out of his skin. Najimy had Dora and Randi, and they had no idea where he had taken them. There'd been no sightings of them by any of the cops on the streets or any other traffic cams that they had access to.

"Where could he be going?" Logan mumbled to himself for the thousandth time. He was at Violet Fullerton's house, waiting to see if the evidence unit found anything inside that might lead them in the right direction. With an MPD detective kidnapped, the combined forces of the District, Maryland, and the FBI had been deployed. There was an FBI chopper in the air, but so far, they had found nothing.

"How can three people just disappear?"

He couldn't just stand around any longer. He started toward his car.

"Hey, where are you going?" Keene fell into step beside him. The younger detective had been keeping a sharp eye on Logan ever since they'd learned Dora was missing. No doubt at Crenshaw's direction. The lieutenant was sharp. He'd give her that. She likely hadn't missed the change in his and Dora's relationship. He was sure she didn't want him going off and doing something stupid. Well, he had to do something. The waiting was going to drive him insane.

"I have to get out there and look for her."

"I'll come with you."

Logan stopped short, examining the young man for several seconds.

"Hey, I want to find her too," Keene said.

"Fine. Let's go."

They jumped into the car. Logan peeled away from the curb.

"Where are we headed, Logan?" Keene asked.

"Dr. Najimy's office."

It hadn't taken long for Crenshaw to get a judge to sign warrants for Najimy's office and home once Roberts found the video. There were already evidence-collection units headed to both locations. Najimy was too smart to keep anything incriminating at his house, where his wife might find it and get suspicious. And he certainly wouldn't have taken any of his victims there. But maybe there was something that could help them at his office where he might have felt it was less likely that anyone would notice. Something that would help them locate Dora.

"We will find her," Keene said with enough conviction that Logan was sure he was attempting to convince himself as well as Logan.

The crime scene investigators were already hard at work when Logan and Keene arrived. The building manager who'd been awakened in order to let them in was fretting in Najimy's waiting room.

Logan hadn't felt this much fear…well, ever. Nearly paralyzing fear. The only thing that kept him moving forward was the knowledge that Dora needed him. Needed him to be strong.

He followed Keene back to Najimy's office. The evidence techs were working, but they hadn't been working the case like he had. They didn't have the insight into Najimy's mind that Logan did.

"I'll take the desk," Logan said, already rounding it. "You search the filing cabinets. We need to get into this computer as well." Logan tapped the silver laptop on the desktop.

"On it," Keene said, pulling his phone out. "Maybe your friend Kaj can come down. That would be faster than transporting the unit to the station."

Logan agreed. He shuffled through the papers on top of the desk, finding only bills for the practice and message slips from Najimy's receptionist. The rest of the desk drawers similarly yielded nothing of interest.

Logan bit back a scream of frustration just as Keene called out from the other side of the room.

"Logan, I think I got something."

"What is it?" Logan crossed over to Keene quickly.

Keene held out a manila folder. Inside were dozens of photographs of their first victim, Monica Gonzalez. From the look of it, she hadn't known she was being photographed.

"That is creepy," Keene pronounced.

Logan couldn't argue that point. He reached for another folder in the same file cabinet. This one had photos of another woman, but Logan didn't recognize her. He and Keene flipped through the folders in the drawer quickly. Folder after folder of photos of women who clearly hadn't known they were being photographed.

"He stalked them," Keene said.

That was exactly what Najimy had been doing. The thought was terrifying. But none of this helped them find Dora.

Keene's phone rang. He answered it on speaker so Logan could here. "Keene, Elkins, the uniforms said you'd taken off from Violet Fullerton's place. Where are you?" Crenshaw barked.

"I couldn't just sit a Fullerton's doing nothing anymore,

so Keene and I headed for Najimy's offices. I figured it was more likely we'd find something here that would tell us where he's taken Dora and Randi." Logan said.

"You're probably right. I'm at the Najimy house now. Mrs. Najimy isn't being very cooperative."

"Then haul her in, in cuffs, and let her sit in the cell. I'm sure that will change her mind," Logan said.

"Have you ever heard the phrase *you catch more flies with honey*?"

Logan was sure that there was nothing sweet about Crenshaw, which might have been why she was having so much trouble getting Mrs. Najimy to talk. No one ever wanted to believe they'd been living with a killer.

"She did tell us that her husband did volunteer work with several drug-rehabilitation programs in the area. I was thinking that could be how he first encountered his victims, since we know Michelle and Monica had problems with drugs and addiction. We'll have to look into that more, but it could be the connection we are looking for."

"Could be," Logan agreed. "But finding Dora is the priority right now. Ask Mrs. Najimy if there is any reason her husband would be headed into Howard County. Any family or friends live out there?"

"Okay, hold on."

The line went silent while Lieutenant Crenshaw was away from the phone. After what seemed like forever, she came back on the line. "No family, but she said her husband used to go out to a cabin in Poolesville when he was working on writing his book a few years back."

A zing of excitement tore through Logan. "What's the address?" He said, moving toward the door already. Keene was hot on his heels.

His phone dinged in answer. "I just sent it to you and Keene."

Keene pulled the text up on the car's navigation system and engaged the map function. "It's about forty-five minutes away."

Logan shot past the elevator bank and to the stairs, not wanting to waste a moment waiting when Dora was in trouble. "Crenshaw, have the locals get out to that address now. Keene and I are on our way."

DORA'S MOUTH WENT DRY. Najimy was the serial killer.

"Don't move," he said. He reached into the SUV's trunk and lowered Randi onto the ground next to Dora. They were in the gravel driveway of a rundown hunting cabin surrounded by woods.

Randi groaned and opened her eyes. Her gaze was unfocused and glassy.

"Don't move," Najimy repeated before rounding the car back toward the front. Dora hadn't seen a weapon, but that didn't mean Najimy didn't have one, and her gun was missing. With her hand still behind her back, Dora worked at loosening the ropes that bound her enough to slip her hands free.

"Randi," she whispered.

Randi turned to face Dora, tears streaming down her face. Dora spared a glance at Randi's bound hands. The rope looked bound tightly. But Randi could run.

Dora lowered her voice even more. "Randi, when I give you the signal, run." She tipped her head toward the trees. "Don't look back and don't stop running."

Randi whimpered again but gave a slight nod.

"Hey, shut up!" Najimy called from the front of the SUV.

"The FBI and the entire MPD are looking for you," Dora

said loud enough for Najimy to hear. "They know where I was headed. They probably have the license plate of this SUV by now, and traffic cameras are marking the route that you took. Your only chance is to let us go."

"Let you go and still go to jail," Najimy called back. "I don't think so."

"If you kill us, you could get the death penalty." Dora could feel the ropes around her wrists loosening now.

"But you will have paid."

"Paid for what? Why are you doing this?"

Just a little more. She just needed Najimy to stay at the front of the SUV. What was he doing up there anyway? She wasn't sure she wanted the answer to that question.

"Because she was innocent, and I couldn't save her." Najimy stepped back around to the back of the SUV.

"Who? Who couldn't you save?"

"My sister. Our father hit her. And me. But she was so small. He killed her. I should've stopped him. I should have—"

"You were young, a victim too. I'm sure you did what you could," Dora said, trying to empathize with Najimy.

For a moment, she'd thought it had worked. But then the soft expression on Najimy's face hardened.

"Enough talk! On your feet, both of you."

"I think Randi is really hurt," Dora said, trying to buy herself more time.

Najimy pulled Dora's gun from his back waistband. "I said on your feet."

Randi whimpered beside Dora. They both struggled to their feet, Dora grabbing a handful of gravel as she did. She flexed her wrist one more time as hard as she could and felt the ropes give just enough that she could pull one hand and then the other out. She held on to the rope so that it would not fall, and Najimy wouldn't realize she was free.

"Move!" Najimy shoved Dora forward toward the cabin. She kept her back angled toward the SUV. She only had a moment before Najimy would realize she was untied.

She threw the gravel at Najimy's face. He screamed. A gunshot blasted through the air. A stinging pain seared Dora's left arm.

"Run," she yelled, already moving in the direction of the trees.

LOGAN HAD CUT the forty-five-minute drive down to a little more than thirty minutes, but he had to slow down once the paved roads gave way to dirt and gravel.

"Here. Turn here," Keene pointed to a narrow drive no wider than a single car's width.

Logan hung a sharp right.

They drove along the rutted road until they turned a corner, and the white SUV came into view.

"This is it," Logan said, throwing the car into Park. "Call it in."

Keene grabbed the radio and began barking out their location and a request for backup. Where the hell were the local cops anyway? There was no time to wait for them.

Logan and Keene got out of the car and went to the trunk.

"I always carry a spare Kevlar for just such an occasion," he said, handing Keene a vest. Logan pulled a second vest over his own head and then grabbed a shotgun out of the sedan's trunk.

"Do you have a spare one of those?" Keene asked, looking pointedly at the shotgun in Logan's hand.

Logan flashed a small smile. "Sorry. This is my baby. My one and only."

"I guess my Glock will have to do." Keene checked that the safety was off, while Logan closed the trunk.

He surveyed the area. Trees to the west, south, and east, with a ramshackle cabin to their north. It looked vacant, but he wasn't taking any chances with Dora's life.

"I'll go right. You go left," he said to Keene. "Keep your eyes open. Najimy has nothing left to lose."

"Got it. You do the same," Keene answered before heading to the left of the cabin.

Logan rounded the right side of the cabin, listening for sounds inside. There was nothing. The exterior windows were coated with too much grime to see inside. He made his way carefully onto the stoop. The front door was unlocked. He pushed it open slowly and had one foot over the threshold when a gunshot ripped through the adjacent woods.

He took off running. *Hang on, Dora. I'm coming. Just hang on.*

BRANCHES TORE AT her slacks, but she heeded her own words and didn't stop running. She pushed through the overgrown foliage and darkness.

"Detective!" Najimy's scream cut through the dense woods.

She slid behind the tree and tried to quiet her breathing. She had no idea how far she'd run or where Randi was. Najimy must have taken her cell phone—not that she'd have gotten service out here anyway. She knew Najimy was out there. Waiting. She couldn't stay there hiding. He wouldn't hesitate to kill her if he found her.

As she made her way around the tree, she saw nothing

but darkness. She moved slowly, hoping the sounds of nature covered whatever noise she might be making.

"Come out, come out, wherever you are."

Najimy's voice echoed off the trees.

She had to move faster. She had to stay alive until Logan came for her. And she knew he would come.

Another gunshot sounded. A hot flash of pain seared through her as she moved, reminding her that she had been shot. How much blood was she losing? Her arm felt as if it was on fire.

"I'm getting tired of this game, Detective. Come out now, and I'll make the end quick."

Dora started moving again, making herself as small as possible.

"There you are." Najimy stepped out in front of Dora, her service weapon in his hand. He had it aimed at her.

Najimy's smile was menacing. "I'm a man of my word." He stretched the gun out farther in front of him. "Goodbye, Detective."

Dora closed her eyes.

A gunshot blasted through the air.

"Dora!"

Dora opened her eyes.

Logan ran toward her just as her legs gave out. He caught her before she hit the ground.

"Randi. She's out there somewhere..."

"We got her. Don't worry—we got her, and she's safe."

"Good. Good. Logan, I love you." His face was the last thing she saw before darkness claimed her.

Chapter Twenty-Three

Was this what death was like? Dora's thoughts raced. After a moment, she realized she was in a soft, comfortable bed. So not dead. That was good. A moment later, she homed in on the sound of snoring. She cracked her eyes open, her gaze landing on a sleepy Logan slumped in a chair next to her bed.

The events from the last several days flooded back into her mind. Chasing the serial killer with Logan. Getting kidnapped with Randi. Getting shot.

The pain of that was still vivid, but whatever the doctors had her on had dulled it enough that she felt a little as if she was floating. It was a strange feeling but better, she supposed, than the alternative. When she opened her eyes again, Logan's were open too and locked on her face.

"Dora!" He leaned forward in the chair and took her hand gently, squeezing it. "Thank God."

He looked awful. His eyes were red rimmed, and his jaw covered in a five o'clock shadow.

She tried to speak but quickly realized her lips were chapped and her throat was raw.

Logan grabbed the empty pitcher from the bedside table and left her long enough to fill it from the attached bathroom. He was back a minute later, filling the glass from the table and lifting it to her lips.

"I should let the doctor know that you are awake," he said.

"Wait." The word cracked out of her. "How long have I been here?"

"A little more than twenty-four hours."

"You look awful."

He laughed and some of the tension eased from his body. "You're one to talk. The bullet went straight through, but you lost a lot of blood." His mouth fell, and he released a ragged sigh. "We thought we'd lost you, Dora. I thought I'd lost you, and it nearly killed me."

"You can't get rid of me that easily," she joked.

But he was not in a joking mood. "I don't want to lose you. Not ever." He cleared his throat, suddenly nervous. "Do you remember what you said to me right before you lost consciousness?"

She remembered, but before she had a chance to answer, the door to the room opened and an older man with olive skin and a white lab coat walked into the room.

"Welcome back to the land of the conscious, Detective Madison. I'm Dr. Hawkins. You gave your friends and coworkers quite a scare there, but it looks like you're going to be just fine."

"Great. When can I get out of here?" she asked.

The doctor chuckled. "Well, not so fast. I want to keep you here for a couple of days, and then we can talk about getting you out of here."

Dora groaned.

Dr. Hawkins simply smiled and went about the business of getting her vitals. He left when he was finished, promising to return later.

Logan came back to her side once the door to the room closed. "I asked you a question before the doctor came in, and you have an answer."

"You did?" she teased. "It must be the drugs. What was the question again?"

Logan smiled and played along. "Do you remember what you said to me before you passed out?"

"After I'd been shot?"

"Yes."

"I'm not sure you can hold a girl to anything she says in the moments after she's taken a bullet."

Logan's face fell. "Does that mean you didn't mean it?"

She could tell he was holding his breath. Dora sobered, gazing at him. "I remember. And I meant it. I still mean it. I love you. I loved you from the moment I met you."

Logan let out a shuddering breath, almost as if he'd been holding it for years. "I was a fool to walk out on you...on us. I didn't know what I wanted or how to want anything, but now I know. I want you. A future with you. A family with you. If that's what you want?"

She looked at him, at the love shining from his eyes and knew. "That's what I want. More than anything, that's what I want."

Logan leaned forward, sealing their declaration with a kiss.

Chapter Twenty-Four

Lisa and Landon stood at the barbecue grill in Dora's backyard arguing over how well to cook the burgers. Layla and Randi lounged on the deck, both with cell phones in hand, debating the next musical selection, having deemed Dora's selections as "too old." Dora didn't mind. In fact, she was happy to see them getting along and hoped that the two girls might even forge a friendship. Noreen had called to say that she'd be late but to save a six pack for her. Dora had it chilling in the refrigerator.

Dora watched from the kitchen, tossing a salad to go along with the food from the grill.

Her family. That was what the people congregating in her yard were. Her family. As much as her mother and Noreen were. And there was nothing she wouldn't do for them. A fierce urge to protect surged in her gut, and she had to tamp it down, reminding herself that there was nothing to protect them from at the moment. At the moment, all was well, and they were safe.

She was still surprised, happily, at how quickly the Elkinses had come to feel like family. She held out her hand, admiring the ring Logan had slipped on it just last week. A square-shaped sapphire rock rimmed by tiny diamonds. There was nothing traditional about it, but that was one of the things she loved most. They'd been through so much, and now this felt like a true new beginning for them. She knew neither of them planned on taking that for granted.

When they'd searched the cabin that Najimy had taken Randi and Dora to, they'd discovered enough evidence to put Najimy away for life. His basement had looked like a house of horrors, and they'd found dozens of desert roses in the greenhouse built into the back of the cabin. The evidence had guaranteed Najimy would face a life sentence, and the prosecutor was confident he'd get a quick guilty verdict when the case went to trial. Najimy's wife had been cleared of any wrongdoing by the justice system, but the court of public approval was a different story. She had to leave DC to get away from the press.

Bruce Najimy had lawyered up and wasn't talking, but a search of his home had answered many of the outstanding questions. He and his sister had suffered abuse at the hands of their father for many years as children. When Bruce had turned eighteen, his father had thrown him out of the house. A month later, seventeen-year-old Sarah's body had been found in a field, badly beaten, a desert rose in her hair. Based on what Najimy had said while he'd held Dora and Randi captive, it seemed as if he had been trying to replace his sister, and when the women he'd kidnapped failed to meet his standards, he had killed them. A sad waste of several young women's lives.

Fortunately for him, John Leonard had recovered from the injuries he sustained in the car accident. Unfortunately, he had been promptly arrested by the FBI for money laundering, among several other charges. It hadn't taken long before he decided to flip on his coconspirators.

Senator Quitoni and his wife had publicly thanked the police department and Dora by name. The arrest had earned her a commendation. The Chief Bayne had taken a two-week victory lap after Dora arrested Najimy, and rumors that he was considering a run for Congress had begun making the rounds. Dora was just glad to have them off her back. And she'd be even happier when she could get back to work. Her wound had healed nicely, and her primary doctor had finally given her the okay to return to the job two days earlier as long as she eased back into field work. As much as she wanted to get back to work, she had to admit she was going to miss her time being on her own.

The experience of being kidnapped had brought them together in a way that neither had been able to explain. Randi still didn't want to go home or reach out to her parents, but she'd agreed to continue living with Violet. Randi had really taken to being a caretaker, doting on Violet and making sure she got to her doctor's appointments and her physical therapy sessions. As thrilled as she was that Randi had found some purpose, Dora wanted to make sure that the teenager had time to just be a teen. She'd begun meeting Randi for lunch at least once a week, and they'd explored the city visiting the museums, taking a cruise on the Potomac, and even hopping on one of those city tour buses and taking the dime-store tour of Washington, DC. And a week ago, Randi had confessed that she was considering signing up for pre-nursing courses at the University of the District of Columbia. Dora couldn't have been prouder and had offered to help her pay for it if she decided to go back to school.

But she'd spent most of her time off with Logan. He'd practically moved into her house. She knew conventional wisdom would have said to take things slowly, but whatever misgivings she'd had about trusting him had faded away over the weeks. Getting shot had put a lot of things in perspective, nothing more so than the fact that time on this earth was precious and shouldn't be wasted. She loved Logan, and she was willing to risk her heart if it meant that she might have a future with him.

Dora smiled as strong arms wrapped around her, pulling her from her thoughts.

"What are you thinking about?" Logan asked.

She didn't want to ruin the day by saying what she'd really been thinking about, so she fibbed. "You."

"Good, because you're always on my mind. And I can't wait to make you, my wife."

They sealed the thought with a kiss.

* * * * *

Harlequin Reader Service

Enjoyed your book?

Try the perfect subscription for Romance readers and get more great books like this delivered right to your door.

See why over 10+ million readers have tried Harlequin Reader Service.

Start with a Free Welcome Collection with free books and a gift—valued over $20.

Choose any series in print or ebook.
See website for details and order today:

TryReaderService.com/subscriptions